LITTLEJIM

Gloria Houston

LITTLEJIM

illustrations by Thomas B. Allen

Philomel Books
New York

The following persons and institutions offered aid in our research to make
both the text and the illustrations authentic representations of the
Appalachian Mountain culture during the time of the setting of this story:
The Appalachian Cultural Center, Appalachian State University, Boone, N.C.
The Rural Life Museum, Mars Hill College, Mars Hill, N.C.
The Tweetsie Railroad, Inc., Blowing Rock, N.C.
Rogers Whitener, syndicated columnist, "Folk Ways and Folk Speech,"
Appalachian State University, Boone, N.C.
J. Myron Houston, local historian, Spruce Pine, N.C.

Copyright © 1990 by Gloria Houston.
All rights reserved. This book, or parts thereof, may
not be reproduced in any form without permission in writing
from the publisher.
Philomel Books, a division of The Putnam & Grosset Book Group,
200 Madison Avenue, New York, NY 10016.
Published simultaneously in Canada.
Printed in the United States of America.
Book design by Gunta Alexander.
The text was set in Perpetua.

Library of Congress Cataloging-in-Publication Data
Houston, Gloria.
Littlejim / by Gloria Houston; illustrations by Thomas B. Allen.
p. cm. Summary: Twelve-year-old Littlejim, a bookish boy
living in a rural North Carolina community in the early years
of the twentieth century, hopes to win a newspaper essay
contest and thus gain the respect of his stern father.
ISBN 0-399-22220-0
[1. Country life—Fiction. 2. North Carolina—Fiction.
3. Fathers and sons—Fiction. 4. Contests—Fiction.]
1. Allen, Thomas B. (Thomas Burt), 1928– ill. II. Title.
PZ7.H8184Li 1990 90-7128 CIP AC [Fic]—dc20
10 9 8 7 6 5 4 3 2

For my daddy,
James Myron Houston

LITTLEJIM

Chapter One

A new year had come to the Creek. The pale winter sun only touched its frosty waters during the middle part of each day. Soon after noonday dinner, the long shadows of the twin peaks the Indians had called the Spear Tops brought twilight to the glens and meadows in the narrow valley hidden deep in the Blue Ridge Mountains.

Each morning Littlejim stood on the porch of the log schoolhouse long before the sun had touched the roof shingles, his breath making smoke in the crisp, clear air. He listened as Mr. Osk, his thin, bespectacled teacher, made his weather forecast for the coming day.

"The twelve days of Christmas foretell the weather for the coming year," said his teacher. "Three days of snow. Then one of wind. Two of rain, then one milder with some sun. Now see the sun's rising for today. Looks like a good year. Early spring, good weather for crops. What with our boys off fighting the Kaiser and all, that'll be good news to everyone on the Creek."

"How do you know all these things?" asked Littlejim.

"It's in the almanac," said Mr. Osk. "Right there in the book. Bigjim's sure to have one. He always plants his crops by the signs."

"I'll ask Papa to let me look at his tonight," said the boy.

Littlejim remembered the thin volume, with *Barker's Almanac* written on the cover, which his father kept hidden behind the big clock on the mantle in the front room. He had watched down the narrow stairwell as Bigjim struggled to read it or the *Star* by lamplight, following the words with his fingers. Sometimes he had seen Mama stop her mending and offer to read aloud to her tall husband, but his papa always put the book away quickly.

Mr. Osk threw one gartered arm over Littlejim's shoulder and guided the boy into the dimly lighted room which buzzed with the sound of young voices. Littlejim knew that Mr. Osk was actually Mama's cousin, Oskar, but since he was the teacher, Mama had told both Littlejim and Nell in her lilting voice, "You vill call him by a term of respect. He is 'Mr.

10

Osk' to you from now on." So Mr. Osk he was to every student in the school, including Littlejim and his sister, Nell.

"Pupils. Pupils," Mr. Osk tapped his stick on the top of his desk set on a platform at the front of the room near the black iron stove. It was time for the day of classes to begin.

Soon Littlejim had finished his lessons. He had finished first and used the time to draw. He was trying to draw the Tigris and the Euphrates rivers with all the cities located in the Fertile Cresent from his geography book with the blue cover.

Then he changed his mind. Paper was too precious to waste, and this day Littlejim wanted to draw something very special. He wanted to draw his papa's big Percherons. Scott and Swain were as fine a matched team of horses as the Henson Creek folk had ever seen. Littlejim dreamed of the day he would be full grown, so he could be a logger and have a team just like Scott and Swain. Together he and Bigjim would cut and haul the big logs from up on Double Head to Uncle Bob's sawmill.

Bigjim was the finest logger on the Creek, and Littlejim was very proud of his father. But he knew that Scott and Swain could share part of the credit. Their huge legs and strong broad backs could snake the biggest chestnut logs out of a laurel thicket. Their

11

strength was great enough to pull the pole wagon loaded with lumber from Uncle Bob's sawmill up the steepest hills on the River Road to the railroad station in Spruce Pine. When they were brushed and curried of a Sunday morning, they looked fine enough to pull the box wagon where Bigjim, Mama, Littlejim, Nell and Baby May rode all the way to Papa's church at the foot of the creek.

Littlejim was might nigh as proud of the big gray horses as his papa was. This day he wanted his drawing to be the one Mr. Osk displayed above the chalkboard as the best drawing of the week. That way every pupil in the school would know that his papa, Bigjim Houston, had the finest team ever seen in the Blue Ridge Mountains of North Carolina.

"What you drawing?" asked Ivor Vance, one of the older boys, over his shoulder. Ivor peeked around to see if Mr. Osk had heard him.

"I'm drawing Scott and Swain," whispered Littlejim to the taller boy. "I wish I had some fancy colors. I could make them ever so pretty. What are you going to draw?"

"I'm going to draw an autymobile," said Ivor. "My uncle says he's going to buy one."

"How you gonna do that?" said Littlejim. "You've never seen one!"

"Well, I heard all about it when my daddy went to Spruce Pine to catch the train," boasted Ivor.

"What was it like?" asked Littlejim.

"It was like a wagon or a carriage, so's my pa says, except no horses were pulling it," said Ivor.

"How can a wagon go without a team to pull it?" puzzled Littlejim.

"I don't know," said Ivor. "But my pa says it went down the road just as pretty as you please. And my uncle says he's going to buy one."

"Well, I want a team like Scott and Swain to pull my wagons when I grow up," said Littlejim. He lifted his paper to puff the erasings off the corner with his breath. He admired his work. Ivor scrunched up his mouth and closed one eye.

"You're mighty good with that pencil," said Ivor. "Mr. Osk is sure to put your picture up today." Then he crumpled his own drawing. He was better at figures, and he knew all the history dates by heart.

Littlejim squirmed. Praise from an older boy was rare, especially from Ivor, who was best at almost every activity at the one-room school. Littlejim tried not to be too proud.

"Better not do that," said Littlejim. "Paper's scarce as hen's teeth, what with the war and all, so's my papa says. Use my eraser."

13

Chapter Two

Just then the door of the schoolhouse flew open. A gust of wind sent Littlejim's drawing fluttering to the floor.

Every pupil in all the neat rows between the windows that lighted each side of the one-room school looked at the doorway. Susie Dellinger threw herself into the room, pigtails flying and petticoats showing where her homespun dress and apron were turned up. Her breath came in gasps.

"Mr. Osk. Mr. Osk, they's a . . ." she said.

A noise louder than thunder came through the door. *Ker-chug. Ker-chug. Wheep,* came the sound. *Ker-chug. Ker-chug. Wheep.*

Books, slates, chalk, papers and pencils flew as every student ran to the roadside windows. Two of the older boys ran out the door. Mr. Osk was frantic.

"Pupils! Pupils!" he clapped his hands. "Children, wait a minute! What on earth is it?"

14

"Hit's a buggy!" wheezed Susie. "But it ain't got no horses pulling it!"

"It's the devil, it is," yelled Andy Pittman, pushing his way through the door to the porch steps.

"Do tell. Do tell," said Jo Rhyne, a quiet upper-grade girl. Her eyes were as big as moons.

"What is it?" asked Littlejim, jumping up and trying to see over the shoulders of the taller boys who stood in the doorway.

"Do tell. Do tell," was all that Jo could say.

Littlejim ran to stand by Mr. Osk. The boy shivered from the cold, but he hardly noticed.

Nell and her friend, Emma Shoop, pulled themselves up on the window sill beside the teacher. They knocked over the cans of plants growing on the shelf. Mr. Osk did not seem to notice.

"What is it making such a racket?" Littlejim asked Andy McGuire, his best friend at school, as they edged their way through the smaller children.

"Why, it's an autymobile," said Mr. Osk. "I've seen pictures of them in the *Star,* but I've never laid eyes on a real one. This must be the first one on the Creek."

The automobile chugged on, rounded the turn and headed into the schoolyard. Littlejim could see it looked like Papa's box wagon, except that it had skinny black wheels and no horses were pulling it. It had a brass lantern hanging out on each side of the front of the box. Littlejim stared at the strange wagon.

"Why, Papa's Percherons would be useless to pull such a wagon," Littlejim told Andy, but Andy continued to stare, his mouth open wide.

Ker-chug. Ker-chug. Wheep. Bang!

Some pupils ran back to their desk. A few of the girls grabbed their coats from the hooks by the door. Nell and Emma jumped down from the window sill. Littlejim followed Mr. Osk through the door.

"It's the devil," yelled Andy Pittman, who ran back through the door and dived under his desk, his long legs sticking out behind him.

"But it won't go," insisted Susie, not believing what her eyes could see. "It ain't got no horses!"

Carl Hicks, the tallest boy in the school, wandered out and pushed his way through the smaller children.

"Why, it's a mocolotive, just a wee mite smaller than the one at the railroad station at Cranberry," said Carl. He was usually the boy who knew everything.

"But then again, it ain't got no tracks," he said. "It can't be a mocolotive." He scratched his head in wonder and moved out to meet the vehicle. The automobile chugged up to the door of the school. Dust fogged the children's eyes as the vehicle came to a stop.

The dust settled, and two figures covered by white canvas coats could be seen sitting in the front of the wagon. One of them wore a huge white hat with a veil. The other wore a little cap. Both of them wore goggles.

The students in Mr. Osk's class stood as silent as if they had no voices and stared at the miracle before them. Mr. Osk came to his senses first. He hurried to help the figure in the white hat down from the strange vehicle.

She unwound the veil of her hat and lifted her goggles.

"Oh, Miz Vance, why, good morning. My! My! This is an occasion!" Mr. Osk was running around like a chicken with its head cut off. The students laughed at him. Nell and Emma jumped up and down, clapping their hands.

The driver took off his goggles and then removed his cap. He stood up in the automobile.

Ivor nudged Littlejim with his elbow. He looked mighty proud.

"That's my uncle's new autymobile," he said. "Told me he was going to get one. I guess I'll get to ride in it, probably today or tomorrow."

Littlejim wished his Uncle Bob would get an automobile so he could ride in it, too.

"I wish . . ." he began.

18

The driver interrupted.

"Ug-um," he cleared his throat.

"Mr. Osk, pupils, Mrs. Vance and I have come all the way up the Creek today to announce an essay competition."

Mr. Vance took a little bow.

"We will give a prize to the pupil who writes the best essay on the topic, 'What it means to be an American.' We will give a fine prize, courtesy of my store, T. B. Vance's General Merchandise, the finest store in Plumtree, North Carolina."

Littlejim hardly heard a word the man said. He was busy looking at that wonderful wagon.

"And we will enter the essay in the competition at the *Kansas City Star*. Students in several states will be competing. The first prize there is ten dollars, and the *Star* will publish the best essay in their July Fourth edition. What do you think of that?" Mr. Vance looked mighty proud of his announcement. Littlejim came to his senses with the words *Kansas City Star*.

Mrs. Vance stood on the ground at the bottom of the steps. She looked at the children gathered around her and smiled at them.

"Is anybody interested in the competition?" she asked, pointing to one student, then another. "How about you, Addie Barrier? I know you'll want to enter, Helen Hughes."

19

Emma and Nell jumped up and down. "Me, too! Me, too!" they giggled.

"Of course, you will," smiled Mrs. Vance at the smaller children. She turned to Littlejim and Ivor, who stood to one side. "And you, Ivor. I guess you should enter. You are in our family, but we won't be the only judges. And you, Littlejim Houston. You will want to enter, Littlejim. You are so good at writing and recitation."

Littlejim didn't answer. In his mind he was already seeing a rare smile lighting his father's face as he read the essay his only son had written right there in print in the *Kansas City Star*.

Ivor nudged Littlejim in the ribs.

"Well, are you, Littlejim?" Mrs. Vance asked again.

"Why, why, uh, yes, ma'am," he said. He had no idea what Mrs. Vance's question was, but he did remember his manners. Mama would be upset if he did not use his manners.

"How about the rest of you?" she said.

Twenty-four hands shot up. Littlejim raised his hand, too.

"Children. Children."

Mr. Osk fluttered across the bottom step of the stairs. "Of course, our pupils will be only too happy to be in the competition, won't we?" he said.

"Yes. Yes," the answers all came at once.

20

"My lovely wife, Elvira, and young Preacher Hall will judge the competition, along with Mr. Osk, of course," said Mr. Vance, with a nod toward the teacher.

"The winning essay will be read next summer at the July Fourth celebration on the Grassy Ridge Bald by the writer," finished Mr. Vance. Then he shook hands with Mr. Osk and helped Mrs. Vance into the seat of the automobile. She tied the veil around her hat, ready to go. Finally her husband stepped around to set the crank.

When he was again seated behind the steering lever, he pulled his goggles down and called to Mr. Osk.

"Give the starter a twist, will you, Osk?" he said. Mr. Osk stepped up to the metal rod sticking out in front of the automobile's hood. He gave a mighty twist.

Nothing happened. Mr. Osk heaved his shoulders to turn the crank again. Still nothing happened. Every student leaned forward as if to help. Mrs. Vance frowned. Mr. Osk twisted the crank again. *Bang!* The automobile sounded like a shotgun. Littlejim covered his ears. The younger children jumped back. It began to sputter and chug. The engine started. Mr. Vance turned the steering lever and chugged off down Henson Creek Road.

21

The class at Mr. Osk's school watched intently.

"My uncle's new autymobile. Guess I'll ride in it today," boasted Ivor.

"It won't go," insisted Susie Dellinger, still not believing her eyes and ears. "It ain't got no horses."

"It's the work of the devil," screeched Andy Pittman, from his hiding place safe under his desk in the back of the classroom.

"It's a wonder," said Littlejim. "It's a wonder. I want one of them someday."

Mr. Osk rubbed his shirt-sleeved arms as he herded the students back into the schoolroom. "Children. Children, in our excitement most of us forgot our coats. Put on your coats and gather around the stove to get warm. We must get back to work in a few minutes. My, my, after all this excitement, will we be able to do our lessons, do you think?" He was still fluttering.

"I know. Let's write a story about this wonder that has come to visit us this day," he said. "Or maybe some of you would rather draw a picture of that fine autymobile. And we have to think of the essay contest. My, my, we have so much to do. I think we should start with a story or a drawing."

All the students gathered around the stove began to talk at once.

All except Littlejim. He went to his desk and

picked up the drawing of Scott and Swain. He turned the paper over so he had a clean sheet.

"What are you doing, Littlejim?" asked Ivor, returning to his desk.

"I'm drawing," Littlejim answered.

"I think I'll draw *my* uncle's fine new autymobile," said Ivor.

"I'll draw the fine autymobile I'll have someday," said Littlejim.

His hands set to work, using his pencil ever so carefully.

Over in the corner, Susie Dellinger stared out the window.

"It'll never go," she insisted. "It ain't got no horses!"

But Littlejim heard nothing. As he drew, his mind was repeating, "What does it mean—to be an American?"

He looked around the classroom. Everyone was hard at work. "I guess we are all Americans, all of us who live on the Creek." But he wasn't sure what that meant.

Chapter Three

Zip. Zip. The plane made smooth cuts across the small strip of wood Littlejim held in his papa's vice. In his mind he could see the waterwheel he was building. He could see the clear water of the Bad Branch turning the wheel as it turned faster and faster.

Littlejim often saw pictures in his mind, and those pictures included all the things he wanted to build, especially that little waterwheel. Now that he had his own woodworking tools he could create all the things he saw in his mind. Once he had thought that if he could build something very fine, he would win Papa's approval and his father would think he was a man. Now he knew better. He built things because it made him feel so good in his heart. But, he thought, if his papa saw words his son had written in the *Kansas City Star,* then he would surely be proud of his son.

Before Christmas he had not been able to work on

24

his waterwheel since the day last fall when Papa caught him using the tools in the shed where they were stored. Bigjim had given his son a switching for messing with his fine woodworking tools.

"My tools," said Bigjim, between lashes of the willow switch on Littlejim's skinny legs. "My tools are for to do a man's work. No call for a fool boy to think they're play-purties. You durstn't touch them again. This'll teach you."

Littlejim bit his lip to keep back the tears until Papa left the woodshed to put a big lock on his tool-shed door. Then he folded his arms on the stack of stove wood and cried. His legs still stung every time he remembered that day.

He heard a voice through his thoughts.

"Jimmy. Jimmy. Where are you?" called Mama.

Littlejim could see just the top of her dark curly head over the washbasin beside the kitchen door.

"Right here, Mama," he called. He carefully placed each of the tools into its place inside the small metal box.

"My little love, I need a cabbage head from the root garden, and a slice of ham from the smoke-house," Mama sang out. She usually sounded as though she were singing. Her speech had a lilt, a sing-song quality that was different from the flat twang of most of the voices of the Creek folk.

"Coming, Mama," he called.

Littlejim hid the box on the top of one of the rafters of the woodhouse. Then he ran up the hill to the door and into the kitchen. Onions, bunched in bouquets of white globes, hung from the rafters. Strings of beans that were dried in their hulls, the kind the mountain people call "leather britches," hung beside them. Long strings of dried apples hung from the frame of the window, making a fragrant curtain of brown dapples as the evening sun shone through them and giving the kitchen a warm, pungent smell. A wreath of shiny red peppers hung near the outside door.

Nell sat in the corner by the big, black cookstove. She was swallowed in one of Mama's aprons. Her little fingers struggled to push the big flat needle through the hard rinds of the orange pumpkin slices. The tabletop was almost covered with slats of pumpkin to be strung, then hung up to dry. Mama would make pumpkin pies from the slices of dried pumpkin. Littlejim's mouth watered when he thought of Mama's pumpkin pies.

"Why are you drying pumpkin this time of year?" he asked.

Mama shook the grate of the cookstove. "Some of the pumpkins in the root cellar started to rot, probably from the warm rains. We must not let good food go to waste."

26

Littlejim handed her three sticks of stove wood from the woodbox standing beside the outer door.

"Thank you, Jimmy. Bring me the buttermilk from the springhouse first, please. I must get the cornbread into the oven. Jim is always hungry when he comes in from the woods. Hurry now."

Mama stood on tiptoe to kiss Littlejim's head. He was taller at twelve years than she was. But he still liked to have Mama kiss the lock of dark brown hair that usually hung down over his eyes.

Littlejim rushed out the door and ran down the path to the springhouse.

He pushed the door open. The moss on the rocks beneath his feet was slippery. Carefully, he lifted the cloth cover from the brown pitcher of buttermilk and picked it up. He peeked under the wooden cover of the butter box, cooled by the tiny spring that trickled through the dark dampness. Nine round balls of butter lay cooling on the board.

Mama saved the extra butter she made from the milk of Old Jerse, the cow, and the eggs from her Dominiquer hens to trade for extras at Mr. Burleson's store. Usually, Mama used the butter and egg money to buy special treats for Littlejim, Nell and Baby May just as she had done the last time they went to the store. She bought cocoa for hot chocolate and white flour for sweet cakes, cookies and gingerbread. Sometimes, she bought a fuzzy brown coconut for Littlejim to shred the white meat for holiday cakes. Often she spent her butter and egg money for fabric to make the children new shirts and dresses.

"Soon I'll have my little waterwheel made. It will look just like the big one that runs the big saws at Uncle Bob's sawmill. Then I can see how fast the Bad Branch will make it run," said Littlejim to the stream that bubbled up from the ground, then ran under the far wall of the springhouse. "I surely would like to finish it soon, but this week I guess I'll have to work at the sawmill." Bigjim liked for his son to work in the sawmill, but he felt that Littlejim was too old to help with women's work in the house.

"'Tain't manly," Bigjim's voice growled through his mustache.

Littlejim liked to help Mama. He often wished his papa were more like his mama, but that was not to be.

Chapter Four

Littlejim walked into the house. "Come, butter, come," he sang as he carried the pitcher of buttermilk into the warm kitchen.

Nell began to sing the little song Mama always sang as she churned the butter.

"Come, butter, come!
Come, butter, come!
Jimmy wants hotcakes,
Nell wants jelly bread."

Mama and Littlejim joined in the chorus, "Come, butter, come!"

Mama was sifting the yellow corn meal into the large wooden bread bowl. She took the pitcher from her son's hands and poured buttermilk into the corn meal. She stirred the mixture and poured it into the sizzling black skillet. Littlejim wrinkled up his nose. Nothing that he could think of smelled quite as good as cornbread browning in ham drippings.

"My little love," said Mama. "Bring me a slice of ham and a cabbage head. Oh, yes, get a few potatoes, too. When you get back, you can help Nell string the pumpkin. We need to clear the table before supper time." Mama was busy and as excited as she always was at supper time. Her words were all run together.

Littlejim took the basket from its hook by the door. Mama and Nell began to sing again.

"I got a gal who lives in Letcher,
Hey, dee ding dong, diddle alley day.
She won't come and I won't fetch her.
Hey, dee ding dong, diddle alley day."

Littlejim whistled the same tune as he walked along the path to the root garden. He pushed back the straw that he and Papa had heaped over the potato hills last fall. First they had mounded the soil where each potato plant marked the bounty hidden below, safe from freezing with first frost.

Littlejim dug into the potato hill with his hands and brought up several potatoes, soil still clinging to their brown skins. He knocked the soil off with his fingers and threw them into the basket.

Then he turned to a large square area covered with straw. The cabbages had been buried in the soil with their heads down and their roots sticking up through the straw.

30

Littlejim laughed out loud. The cabbages were all lined up in straight rows. They looked like the soldiers he read about in Papa's *Kansas City Star* who were fighting far away in Europe. But these cabbage soldiers were standing on their heads. He gave them a salute, like the one Uncle Bob gave to Ive Lusk when Ive came to the sawmill in his soldiering clothes.

Littlejim pulled a cabbage head from the ground, slung it over his shoulder by the root and picked up the basket of potatoes. He began to whistle as he watched the sun go down between the twin peaks of the Spear Tops. In winter, the sun left the Creek in the gap between the two peaks. In summer, it moved farther west, to set over the Little Bald Mountain.

The dry leaves in the thicket by the path from the garden rustled their music with his whistle-tune. The wind soughed through the white pines on the side of the hill behind the white-trimmed green house Bigjim had built for his family.

Littlejim was still whistling as he turned the corner in the path. His father stood there.

"Get a move on, boy," Bigjim growled. "You're slow as molasses in January." Bigjim's eyes were like gray winter skies under his slouch hat. His beard and overalls were covered with wood chips that bore testimony to his day in the woods.

"They's milking to be done. And slopping the

31

hogs," said the voice that cracked like a whip. "Don't need no woolgathering lazies here. Time you acted like a man."

Littlejim's whistle faded. The winter skies seemed to cloud over. The sun was gone behind the peaks.

"Yes, sir," said Littlejim as he hurried into the safety of the smokehouse. Bigjim was a hard taskmaster. And he was a tough man to please. "This time I will," the boy said half aloud. "If only Papa could see my essay in the *Star*."

He slammed the door as he walked into the kitchen and handed his mother the thick slice of ham. She started it sizzling in the black iron skillet as Littlejim washed the potatoes in the gray enamel pan and trimmed the cabbage, dropping the outer leaves into the bucket for the hogs.

"Papa's home," he said.

Mama selected a red pepper from one of the strings hanging on the kitchen rafters. She began to slice the potatoes.

"He will be hungry, tired and cold. Nell, clean up the pumpkin and shred the cabbage, please."

Littlejim hated to leave the smells of frying salt-cured ham and cabbage. So he managed to wait a few minutes longer by slicing the potatoes. Finally, he took the slop bucket filled with kitchen scraps from its place on the back porch and carried it carefully to the hog pen.

Littlejim counted five hogs. One sow and four shoats lazily moved toward the trough. The shoats would soon be ready for late butchering to resupply the smokehouse with ham and bacon. The winter supply never seemed to last through the summer. Bigjim always butchered the shoats as late in the winter as possible, but February would be too late. By that time, there was too little cold weather to allow time for curing. The warm days of spring would cause the meat to spoil if it was not cured. This year Littlejim was old enough to help with the late butchering. Bigjim had promised.

He slowly poured the slop into the trough and watched as the hogs jostled one another to get the largest portion. Lilac, the sow, put all four feet into the two-sided wooden box with a bottom shaped like a V. Lilac knew all the tricks. She had the most experience. She had lived longer. Bigjim would not butcher Lilac because she was needed to provide new pigs for the following year.

After shucking an armload of dried corn from the corncrib, the boy threw the ears into the swill and mud. The hogs pushed against one another to get to the corn. Littlejim leaned over the fence and scratched one of the shoats beneath the ear. The enormous animal rubbed his back against the fence post that leaned into the pigpen and grunted his satisfaction.

"Jimmy," called Mama from the back porch. "Supper's on the table. Milking can wait. Wash your hands."

Chapter Five

At dark the family sat around the supper table in the big kitchen, the fire from the cookstove warming Bigjim's back.

"Papa," said Nell. "Is Littlejim going to win the essay competition? Do you think he will get to give his speech at the singing next summer on July Fourth?"

Littlejim stopped his fork loaded with ham and cabbage in midair. He watched his father with eyes wide with fear. Even Baby May in her highchair made of laurel twigs stopped digging her spoon into her cup of cornbread softened in sweet milk to look at her father. Milk trickled down her chin. Mama wiped it off.

Bigjim placed his knife and fork on the table. He poured some coffee from his big cup into the saucer, lifted the saucer to his lips to cool it by blowing on it and finally drank it down. Across the cherry table, Mama closed her eyes and sighed. Try as she might, she had never been able to stop her husband from sassering and blowing his coffee. Then he pushed back his chair and wiped his mustache on a coarse napkin. The children had not moved since Nell spoke. Even Mama sat quietly, her hands in her lap.

"What competition do you be meaning?" intoned Bigjim. "You know full well that I don't hold with my family a-making plumb fools of theirselves by speaking in front of their neighbors." He leaned back in his chair. His dark eyes glistened in the soft light from the kerosene lamp in the center of the table.

"My son disobeyed me and made his speech at the Christmas tree, knowing I am displeased with sich goings-on. What essay air you talking about now?" said Bigjim.

Nell began to talk quickly, her words running into one another in her haste. "Today Mr. and Mrs. Vance came driving up to the school in a wonderous autymobile without any horses to make it go."

"Spawn of the devil, them contraptions," spat Bigjim, folding his arms tightly to his chest. "Go on, child."

"Well, Papa. They asked Mr. Osk if we could write an essay and enter it into a competition. They

36

are giving a prize and the winner gets to make a speech at the July Fourth singing next summer. Mrs. Vance even said Littlejim might win and it might be printed . . ."

Littlejim interrupted his sister. "She only asked me if I wanted to write an essay. She didn't say I might win."

"She as good as said . . ."

"That true, boy?" Bigjim turned to face his only son.

"Well, sir. She asked me if I would like to enter. That's all," answered his son. Littlejim knew better than to let his father know how important entering the competition was to him.

Bigjim put his elbows on the table. Mama shook her head and sighed. But his father continued to stare at the boy. One long finger shot out in Littlejim's direction and pointed at his son.

"Don't let me hear of you a-wasting your time with such tomfoolery. You have work enough to do around the farm with me away so much. Besides, they's a war goin' on across the seas. It ain't fittin' to be frolicking when our men from right here on the Creek are dyin' in a war and all. My son darsn't disobey me again to make a fool of hisself. Do you mind what I say?"

Bigjim had spoken. His family knew that to argue

37

was of no use. He picked up his knife and fork, speared a piece of ham, and pushed some cabbage onto the fork with his knife. But before he could get the food to his mouth, Mama pushed herself up to her full height in her chair. Even then, Mama's head was hardly as high as Littlejim's skinny twelve-year-old shoulders.

"James," she said sternly, "how will our son's essay or his making a speech affect the war with the Kaiser? Now that I'd like to know."

Mama looked just like one of her Dominiquer hens who got all puffed up and mad when Nell and Littlejim tried to rob the nest of eggs. Her cheeks were very red. Talk of the war with the Kaiser upset Mama. Her parents had come from Germany when she was only a little girl.

"When the children were little, I held to your Freewill beliefs. They are older now. It is not fullsome that they should not be a part of the church and community doings like other folks."

Littlejim watched his parents' faces, while keeping his own blank. He could not allow Papa to see his disappointment. Papa held to the Freewill beliefs, even though he hardly ever went to church. Most Sundays he spent hunting or jawing with the other Creek men. The Freewill Church was called by some the "footwashing" Baptists, because they sometimes had a service where it was told up and down the Creek that they washed each other's feet like Mary Magdalene had washed the feet of Jesus. Littlejim wondered if that was true.

Mama attended the Missionary Baptist Church up at the head of the Creek almost every Sunday morning. Usually she took the children with her. Bigjim rarely went to church, but when he did, the whole family went with him.

The only time Littlejim had ever heard his parents "have words," as Mama said, those words had drifted up the loft stairs from the front room after his parents had gone to bed one Sunday night. They were angry words. The words he had heard were "Freewill" and "Missionary."

Littlejim looked around the table at Nell and Mama and Baby May, all sitting very still. Then Bigjim pushed his chair away from the table.

"Gertrude," thundered Bigjim. The children jumped. Papa had never yelled at Mama before. He yelled at them, but never at his tiny wife.

"Gertrude," he said again. "I will not hold with young'uns of mine a-wasting their time with tomfoolery and a-making plumb fools of theirselves. Last time it was holding Christmas celebrations in that house of God. That is over and done with, but this family won't be a part of sich again."

39

Bigjim glowered across the table at his tiny wife. Mama seemed to get taller in her chair.

"James, the church we attend had nothing to do with this. Our boy has a way with words. He is a born scholar. Osk told me so. It's sinful for him not to enter the competition. My fadde taught us a man should use his talents or he would lose them."

Bigjim stood up. At better than six feet, he towered over his family table.

"What's sinful about it?" boomed Bigjim. "Why, womern, he's a-making a plumb fool of hisself in front of the whole Creek with speeches and sich. A boy his age should be out a-working on the farm, a-cutting timber and a-hunting, not doing womern's bookish things. He should be a-doing manly things. Of course, it ain't like he was *much* of a man."

"Of course, he's not much of man, James," she said, quietly. "He has only seen twelve summers."

"When I had seen twelve summers, I was a head taller than he is and I didn't have time for books. I was already in the woods making man's wages," Bigjim muttered.

Littlejim had heard his papa tell of the hardships of his youth so many times he could almost repeat the story by heart. That did not make his father's words about him any easier to hear.

Bigjim pushed back his chair. His face seemed

40

carved in stone. He walked to the door of the front room. "I'm a-going to read the *Star*. It come today, I reckon."

Bigjim was proud that he received the *Kansas City Star* every week. Reading it gave him an opinion to say when the men gathered at Uncle Bob's sawmill to settle up on Saturday or at the jawing of a Sunday morning. Littlejim often watched by the light of the kerosene lamp as his father labored to figure out the words. Papa had only finished the Primer at school, and his son knew that reading was hard work for him.

Littlejim looked across the supper table at Mama, then at Nell. Two tears slowly slipped down his little sister's cheeks. Mama was still chewing although she had no food in her mouth. Baby May had stopped slurping her bread and milk.

"Littlejim," said Nell. "Why didn't you tell Papa about the *Star*? That might have made him let you write the essay."

"What about the *Star*?" asked Mama.

"The winner of the essay competition for the whole country will be printed in the *Star*. I really would like to have something I wrote printed where Papa would see it," said Littlejim. "I have decided to write the essay, no matter what Papa says." He swallowed hard. His heart was flying inside his chest. He

41

had never dared to defy his father before and now he feared Mama's disapproval, too.

"That would be a great achievement," said Mama. "I would be very proud to have my son's speech printed in a fine newspaper like the *Star*. James would think that a fine thing, too, I believe."

"The other prize is ten dollars, and that's a lot of money," said Littlejim. "I could maybe buy my own team so I could help Papa in the woods."

"Or ten dollars could be used to send my fine scholar of a son away to school where he could learn all his mind could hold," said Mama.

Littlejim had never thought of that. He had always dreamed of being a logger like his papa.

"And you get a Bible, too," said Nell. "Mr. Vance is going to give it."

"I already have a new Bible," said Littlejim. "I won that at the Christmas tree. I would give the Bible to you, Nell, so you could have one of your very own."

Nell smiled shyly at her big brother across the table. "Goody, Littlejim. You are sure to win, and I won't say a word to Papa, either."

"Jimmy, you are a scholar. It is fitting that you should enter the competition. We will have to find a way around your father's stubbornness. You must not be angry at your father, my little love. He misses his lack of schooling sorely. We shall see what we can do. Now finish your good dinner. I did not cook this good food to feed to Lilac!"

Littlejim picked up his fork. He felt encouraged. He knew in his heart that he had to write the essay, but if Mama thought he should, too, then he had to find a way to enter the competition.

Chapter Six

The following evening, Littlejim carried the lantern in one hand, and the metal pail filled with milk in the other. As he opened the kitchen door, Mama and Nell were finishing the dishes.

"But why does Papa have to be so mean to Littlejim?" asked Nell. Littlejim had been wondering about that same question all day at school.

"Woolgathering, Jimmy?" Mr. Osk the schoolmaster had asked. "That isn't like you, Jimmy. Where are you today?"

Littlejim had felt his face getting redder and redder. He was Mr. Osk's star pupil at the little Henson Creek school, and he took great pride in his studies. But that day his mind had been on his father and on trying to decide if he was really brave enough to defy his papa and enter the competition.

"Why doesn't Papa understand?" mumbled Littlejim, setting the pail of milk on the dry sink.

44

"Your papa is a hard man, yah," said Mama. Her lilting speech grew stronger when she was upset. "Life has not been kind to your papa. He had no time to be a kinder—a child—when his father died so young. James had to go to the woods instead. He never learned to play."

"But he always scolds Littlejim for everything," said Nell. "Why doesn't Papa want Littlejim to have any fun?"

Mama tied a clean white cloth to the bail on each side of the milk pail. Then she tilted the pail to strain the milk through the cloth into a pitcher. Finally, she set the pitcher on the back of the cookstove to clabber. Tomorrow she would churn the clabber for butter. Mama wiped her hands on her apron after she had rinsed the pail and turned it up to drain on the dry sink.

"We shall make our fun tonight. Don't worry. Nell, bring out the white flour and sugar. We'll make some cookies," said Mama.

She took some butter from the cut-glass butter dish, added some white sugar and began to beat the mixture as though she was mad at it. Littlejim knew this must be a special occasion. Mama usually made cookies with molasses or honey. White sugar was saved for company.

"Jimmy, crack us some walnuts," she added.

"Oh, goodie. Walnut cookies," said Nell, sticking

her finger into the cookie mixture. Mama removed Nell's hand from the bowl and continued to cream the butter and sugar.

Nell cracked an egg on the side of Mama's brown mixing bowl.

"Tookie. Tookie," said Baby May, banging her wooden spoon on the side of her cradle in the corner by the stove.

"Do you think we could make Papa like Littlejim more?" asked Nell.

"Your papa likes his son," said Mama. "He does not understand why his son is not just like he was as a boy. He forgets that his son is a different person with different talents."

"If he likes me, he has a fine way of showing it," whispered Littlejim under his breath and placing a round black walnut on the flat side of the sadiron he held between his knees. Mama heated the iron on the cookstove to press their Sunday-go-to-meeting clothes after washday. The rest of the time, the sadiron became a nutcracker.

Carefully he held the black rippled nutshell so he would hit it and not his fingers with the old hammer that had one claw broken off. He hit the end of the walnut just right. The two halves fell apart. The goodie in each half was intact. He tapped each half in turn, and picked up two perfect nutmeat halves.

"Maybe, if I practice, I can get them to come out in one piece, like Uncle Bob," muttered Littlejim. Uncle Bob knew just where to tap the thick walnut so that the shell fell away, leaving the nutmeat in one piece. Littlejim had tried and tried, but had never learned the secret to Uncle Bob's trick.

Littlejim picked the pieces of shell out of his bowl of walnuts and dumped the goodies into the batter Nell was stirring.

Mama helped Nell spoon the batter onto the flat black pan. Littlejim shook the grate and added stove wood to the fire. Mama slid the pan into the oven, then she ladled stew from the bubbling pot into a bowl and mashed the vegetables with a fork.

"Maybe, if I hug Papa and tickle him under his beard—he likes that—I can tell him to like Littlejim, too," said Nell.

"Perhaps that would help," said Mama, smiling and kissing her daughter on top of the head. She picked Baby May up from the cradle and began to spoon the stew into the baby's open mouth.

"Jimmy, we will need some stove wood for morning. The woodbox is almost empty. Nell, help your brother bring a load of wood," said Mama. "And put on your shawl, too."

Chapter Seven

Nell took her shawl from the hook by the door. She followed her skinny brother down the path to the woodshed and began to gather long sticks of wood into her little arms.

"Not firewood, Nell. It's too long. Papa cut that for the fireplace. Mama needs stove wood, the short pieces."

Littlejim helped the girl stack stove wood onto both arms. Then he loaded his own.

Inside, the children dumped their loads of wood into the kitchen woodbox. Mama was stirring something in an iron pot on the stove. The sweet fragrance of chocolate filled the room. Mama had sent them for wood so she could bring out the tin of cocoa she kept hidden away for special occasions.

She scooped the skin from the top of the hot milk and poured a mug for each of them. Then she lifted

the walnut cookies one by one to the plate. The three
of them sat at the square kitchen table. Littlejim took
big bites of his cookie. Nell nibbled the brown edges.
In her cradle Baby May held her cookie clutched to
her chest as her head drooped to one side and her
sleepy eyelids closed.

Mama held her cookie in one hand while she
drank from her mug. She had a chocolate mustache
around her upper lip. Nell had one, too. Littlejim
quickly licked his away.

"We should have cookies every night," said Nell.

"Then they wouldn't be so special," said Mama.
"When we have something every day, it becomes ev-
eryday, not so special. We have Papa's lovely hams to
eat at almost every meal. In the old country, ham was
saved for special occasions. We did not have it every
day. That made it a very special food."

The children munched their cookies silently.

"We have your papa's love but he does not show
it every day. He shows it in ways, not in words. That
is what makes his words so special," continued
Mama. "Your papa did not learn to show love in
words when he was a child. He was not given words
and hugs so he does not know how to give them."

"And Papa was very poor," said Littlejim.

"Not always," said Mama. "His father was a gentleman farmer. He owned almost all the bottom land

on this creek. Then the land turned bad. Crops didn't make. Robert left the Creek to find work. That's when your papa left school to work on the farm. He never had the chance to go to school. He misses that, too, I think."

"Did Uncle Bob help Papa learn to log?" asked Littlejim.

"Uncle Bob became a lumberman down below the mountains near Morganton. When he came back to the Creek settlement, your papa went to the woods to learn to cut trees for Uncle Bob's sawmill."

"And Papa's a fine logger," said Littlejim proudly. "Uncle Bob says he's the best in these parts."

"Yah! He is good," said Mama. "He makes a fine living for us all. He shows his love for us in many ways. We have one of the finest houses on the Creek—or the River Road, for that matter. He has built us four fine rooms and a sleeping loft. We have a fine barn, a smokehouse, a woodshed, the spring-house."

Mama counted the buildings off on her fingers.

"We have a root cellar and a privy," said Mama. "And I have the finest cookstove on the Creek. Yah. Your papa is a good man. A fine husband. A good provider. He surely loves us all."

Mama banged her mug on the table as she set it down.

50

"But he does not remember that children need to hear *words* of love and pride! He forgets that his son is a fine scholar and we should be so proud of him!" she said.

Mama looked up, startled. Two pairs of eyes followed her gaze. Bigjim's tall figure loomed in the doorway. He yawned and stretched. Then he walked to the table, took two cookies and tossed both of them into his mouth at the same time.

"Ruining these young'uns again, Gertrude?" he asked.

He took another cookie and ate it in one bite. Taking two more from the plate, he leaned against the doorframe and scratched his back on the corner of the frame.

"Ought to save these fine sweet cakes for Sunday dinner," he said.

Littlejim saw his father's eyes twinkle, and he thought he saw a smile begin through the brown beard. Bigjim seldom smiled, so his son could not be sure. But Littlejim knew that if anything could make the dour man smile, it was Mama's walnut cookies. Bigjim was partial to sweets, especially to Gertrude's "warnet" cookies, as he called them.

"Time for bed," said Mama. She placed the mugs in the dishpan on the water shelf.

She kissed each of the children.

51

"Gute Nacht," she whispered.

"Don't let the bedbugs bite," giggled Nell.

Mama carried the kerosene lamp. Bigjim lifted the cradle where Baby May now lay sound asleep, half her cookie clutched in her hand.

Littlejim and Nell climbed the narrow stairs to the sleeping loft.

"But, James," Mama's voice came up the stairs. "What possible harm could it do our son to write an essay and give a speech?"

Littlejim could not hear the words, but he heard Bigjim's voice rumbling up the stairs.

Finally he heard his father's voice, "Enough, Gert, enough."

Littlejim pulled the quilt Mama had made for him around his ears to keep out the cold. He would have to find a way to enter the essay competition. As much as he did not want to be a disobedient son, he knew he had to if he ever wanted his papa to see that he was a man.

"Littlejim," said Nell through the wall between their rooms in the sleeping loft. "Why does Papa always scold you if he loves you? He doesn't scold me so much."

"I don't know," whispered Littlejim. "Sh-h. Papa might hear you."

"You must find a way to make him let you enter

the essay competition," said Nell, speaking a bit louder. "Maybe I can sing him a song when he comes in from the woods tomorrow. He likes that."

"Good night, Nell," said Littlejim.

"Littlejim," insisted Nell. "I can try . . ."

"Good night, Nell," said her brother again.

In the distance a hoot owl called. Then silence like the snowflakes falling outside the windows soon covered the valley.

Chapter Eight

"Wait, Littlejim. Please wait for me. I can't keep up," Nell panted as she ran down the hill.

But Littlejim took a runny-go, and slid into the mud of the main road, the little wooden sled bouncing behind him.

Nell ran harder.

Finally on the main road, she hobbled up to the sled. One shoe was unbuttoned, and her shawl was falling around her neck.

The *clip-clop* of a horse's hooves and the *skur* of buggy wheels sounded around the bend in the road. Preacher Hall's big bay horse pulled the young minister's new buggy.

"Whoa, there. Howdy, Littlejim. Howdy, Nell. Going to the store?" bellowed the hefty young man through his red beard. He tipped his black hat to Nell.

Nell hid her face behind her big brother's sweater,

and peered around Littlejim's shoulder. She was afraid of this giant of a man who preached hellfire and brimstone on Sunday, then laughed like thunder the rest of the week.

The minister leaned out of his seat, and pinched Nell's icy cheek.

"How be ye today?" He gave the typical greeting of the Creek folk.

"Tolerable well," replied Littlejim, completing the ritual.

"It was gladsome that Bigjim put away his Freewill beliefs and let you young'uns come to the Christmas tree this time. That prime laurel Ive Lusk staked up on Double Head for us might nigh filled up the church, didn't it?" bellowed the big man. "For a spell I didn't know just where we'd put the congregation. I told the deacons we might have to set the pews out in the churchyard."

The preacher's round stomach jostled up and down as he laughed at his joke. But Littlejim was serious.

"It was a proud day for me," said the boy. Littlejim was lost in thought. He remembered how good Christmas felt when he had helped Nell go to the Christmas tree. He remembered how proud Mama looked when he stood up to recite his verses. A smile crept across his face and turned into a wide grin.

Then he frowned. "But you know Papa don't hold with celebrating. He was a mite fussed about my recitation, especially in a church that won't hold to his Freewill beliefs."

"Bigjim sure takes his religion seriously for one who don't practice it," chuckled the parson. "I'll stop by and tell him how proud he ought to be of his fine son next time I howdy him."

"That'ud be mighty good of you, Preacher," said Littlejim. "I wanted to go tolerable bad, and I was glad Nell here got to go, too." He pulled his little sister around beside him, but protected her with his arm.

"Bigjim cuttin' on the Bad Branch today, son?" he asked the boy.

"No, sir. Uncle Bob sent the crew to the Murphy Flat about sunup. He needed Papa's team to snake the logs out today."

"Trying to finish up that job by Saturday, I guess?" the preacher seemed to ask and answer his own questions at the same time. "Lumbering in this country finally beginning to pay off. Ever since Bob bought that Edgar circle saw and set up on the Lusk place."

Littlejim thought they might be in for a sermon right there in the middle of the road from the way the preacher had started.

"Course, with the war on and all," the preacher

57

continued, "the army's buying up every stick of timber a man can cut, I reckon."

Preacher Hall slapped his huge knee. The horse pranced lightly to the side.

"Whoa, Job. Stand still. I want to jaw with these young'uns fer a spell. I reckon it'll take Blue Ridge timber to whup the Kaiser, fer true, I guess." He laughed at his own joke. Littlejim laughed, too. Nell stared at the big man with round eyes.

"Yes, sir," he said. Littlejim shifted from one foot to the other. "I have a job, too."

The parson frowned.

"Bigjim's not taking you into the woods again to do a man's work, is he?"

"No, sir."

"Your pa forgets that you ain't a full-growed man yet. He puts too much on you. Besides, you ought to be in school. Osk tells me you're his prize pupil," said Preacher Hall.

"I'm going to school. I help out afterwards and on Saturdays when Fayette's down in his back. I'm the dust doodler," Littlejim said proudly. "I make ten cents a day."

"My, my," said the preacher. "I'm mighty glad to hear that. Dust doodling is a lot better job fer a boy than snaking logs out of the woods with a team. Twelve years ain't hardly old enough to take on a man's work."

A few snowflakes had begun to fall from the clear blue sky. Littlejim wondered where they came from. They clung to the horse's mane.

"Looks like you're headed to the store today," laughed Preacher Hall. "Sorry I ain't going in your direction. You young'uns better hurry on now."

"Yes, sir," said Littlejim.

"Good day," said the preacher, tipping his hat as his buggy moved away.

"We have to hurry, Littlejim," said Nell, running ahead. "It's snowing harder."

"Wait on me," her brother answered, the little sled following bumpety, bumpety on the road behind him.

They walked in silence. Littlejim's chest seemed to swell as he saw the sunlight shimmer off the ice-glazed branches of the trees. The winter sky was painted a blue so bright it stung his eyes. Here and there a snowflake drifted down. The boy was filled with gladness at the beauty of it all. He felt the way he had felt reciting his verses at the church. He began to run.

"I'll feel that way again," he shouted, jumping into the air and almost turning the sled over. He knew he would find a way.

He ran past Nell toward the River Road.

"Wait for me," shouted Nell.

Chapter Nine

Side by side, they trudged up the steps of the big white building and across the wide front porch.

Littlejim loved the dark cavern that was Burleson's Store. Bigjim often said the store sold everything from stick matches to pianos. There were so many things to see. Fine new saddles, garden hoes, plows, horseshoes, kegs of nails, shiny blue stovepipes, bolts of colored cloth, ladies' bonnets, tinned foods, crocks of spices and jars of candy lined the walls and stood on the counters. In barrels on the floor were displayed dried beans, pickles and strips of salt pork.

Best of all, Littlejim thought, were the smells. Besides the fragrance of leather and kerosene, the store smelled of salt brine from the pickles, cinnamon from the spice shelf and the wonderful, almost-sour smell of the hoop of cheese Mr. Burleson kept in the round wooden crate on the high counter beside the shiny brass cash register. Littlejim liked cheese better than almost anything, even candy.

Sometimes, when a customer's due-bill was paid, the children in that family received a setup. A setup was a piece of free candy or some other treat selected by the child. Each child was allowed to choose a favorite, which Mr. Burleson presented with a flourish as he bowed from the waist. Mama's bill usually had a credit balance from the butter and eggs she traded at the store, so Littlejim and Nell always received a setup whenever they went there.

"What would you like today, my pretty little Nell?" asked Mr. Burleson, as he began to whistle the melody of "Darling Nelly Gray."

Nell blushed, but her blue eyes shone with delight. She stood gazing up at the round jars filled with peppermint sticks, large round jawbreakers and the many colors of jellied fruits. At last she pointed to the jar which held long peppermint sticks spiraled with red and white.

"If you please," Nell whispered shyly, "a peppermint stick."

"One peppermint stick for my pretty little Nell," said Mr. Burleson, walking around the end of the counter and presenting the peppermint stick with a bow and a flourish.

"Why don't you run up to the house and see Annie while I get your mama's order together?" Mr. Burleson asked. "She misses you since her pa moved off the Creek. I'll send Littlejim when the order is ready."

"Thank you, sir," said Nell, as she closed the door and went skipping across the porch holding the precious peppermint stick in front of her.

"And what'll it be today, Jimmy? Candy or a sliver of cheese?" asked the bald man wearing a white apron. The sleeves of his starched white shirt were pushed up and held by garters.

"A piece of cheese, sir, if you please," replied Littlejim.

"I'm partial to cheese myself," Mr. Burleson chuckled. He walked over to the counter where the hoop of cheese was covered by a white wooden crate.

The door opened. Littlejim looked up. Andy McGuire and his father came in, bringing a gust of cold air.

"Where are your ten-penny nails?" Mr. McGuire asked. He said "Wher-rdr air-dr your-dr . . ." Littlejim had to listen carefully to understand the strange pronunciations. They were very different from the usual mountain speech patterns so familiar to Littlejim's ears.

Andy came over to stand with Littlejim as Mr. McGuire made his way to the back of the store.

"Right over there. In the keg behind the plowshares," said Mr. Burleson, as he carefully lifted the top of the round wooden crate and unwound the mesh from the golden wheel. Then he took a long sharp knife and cut two thin slices of cheese. He placed each slice on a small square of brown paper. He reached into a big tin and added two thick white soda crackers to the packets and handed one to each boy.

"Much obliged," said Littlejim.

"Thank you, sir," said Andy with a big smile. He had not expected to share Littlejim's setup.

Wiping his hands on his white apron, Mr. Burleson nodded and walked toward the hardware section to join Mr. McGuire.

Andy and Littlejim walked over to sit on the ledge at the front windows. For a few minutes, they munched in silence.

"How did you like Mr. Vance's autymobile?" said Andy. "I can't figure out how it could go without horses, can you?"

"Mr. Osk told me it was something to do with burning fuel inside the engine," answered Littlejim.

"I looked real close," said Andy. "I didn't see a boiler anywhere nor any place for wood to stoke the fire."

"It can't be run by steam," said Littlejim. "I can't

63

rightly say what makes it run, but it is a wonder."

"Do you reckon," Andy pronounced the "r-dr" as his father had, "that we'll ever get to ride in one of those things?"

"Wouldn't that be a proud day?" answered Littlejim. "To ride in a real autymobile!"

"Sitting tall and splenderous," said Andy.

"Yeah, a proud day," agreed Littlejim.

Mr. McGuire and the storekeeper walked to the door.

"We'd best be goin'," said Mr. McGuire. "What do I owe ye fer my boy's setup?"

"It's on the house. He's a fine boy," said Mr. Burleson.

"Thanks be to ye. Good day," said Mr. McGuire, throwing an arm around his son's shoulders and guiding him out the door.

Littlejim watched the father and son walk across the porch, the boy enclosed in his father's protective arm. A longing took hold of his stomach. "Why isn't Papa like Andy's pa?" he asked himself. His eyes stung. A voice interrupted his thoughts.

"From what Osk tells me, you are quite the scholar," said Mr. Burleson. "He tells me you are his prize pupil."

Littlejim blushed. Bigjim had told him a man ought not be too proud, but he could hardly keep from standing a bit taller and straighter when a fine man like Mr. Burleson offered words of praise.

"Miz Gertrude's order is ready, Jimmy. Did Bigjim and Miz Gertrude have a fine Christmas?"

"No, sir. Papa says it's just another day," said Littlejim.

"Your papa's a fine man, even if he is a mite soured on life," mused Mr. Burleson, as he wrapped the packages with twine. "He needs to work a mite less hard. Him and Bob making a fortune selling the army timber, so's I hear?"

"No, sir. Papa says times is hard, uh, are hard, what with the war and all," said Littlejim.

Mr. Burleson laughed and wiped his hands on his apron. "Your papa would say times was hard if he was in heaven walking streets paved with gold. Bigjim is a tight man with a dollar."

A lady wearing a feathered bonnet came into the store.

"Why, howdy, Miz Addie," said Mr. Burleson. "Littlejim, you tell Miz Gertrude that I'll take all the butter and eggs she can spare for the winter. Hers is the only yellow butter I see from Christmas 'til the spring freshet."

Littlejim smiled. He wouldn't give away Mama's secret. During the cold winter months when Old Jerse's milk made pale white butter, Littlejim had helped Mama with the churning. With her little paring knife, he had watched her scrape a carrot into fine scrapings and set the bowl aside to drain. After a while she mixed the orange-colored carrot juice with the fresh butter, working it with her warm hands until it became a pale yellow. It wasn't the same yellow as summer butter, but it wasn't white, either.

"We eat with our eyes as well as our mouths," said Mama. "Yellow butter seems to taste richer than white. Well, carrots are good food, too."

Mr. Burleson walked with Littlejim to the big front doors and looked out. "Nell went up to play with Annie. You'd better go get her," he said. "The old woman in the sky is picking her geese today."

When Littlejim returned with Nell, Mr. Burleson came outside with a stack of packets in his arms. He set them on the edge of the porch and jumped off. Then he helped Littlejim to pack the sugar, coffee, thread and a tiny precious tin of cocoa into the box on the sled.

Finally he lifted Nell off the high porch. Littlejim took Nell's mittened hand and began the long walk back up the Henson Creek Road. The shoes of the two children made circles on either side of the long solid tracks of the sled.

Chapter Ten

Long before sunup the following Saturday, Littlejim wiped the sleep from his eyes and broke the ice in the washpan on the back porch. Quickly he washed his face and hands. Littlejim had a job to do. Today he would earn a dime working as dust doodler in Uncle Bob's sawmill. Mama always reminded him that the sawmill was a dangerous place, especially when he worked under the big saw. But Littlejim liked to work with the men. Most of all he liked the shiny dime Uncle Bob paid him at the end of his day there.

He hurried to the kitchen and quickly ate Mama's fried sidemeat, sawmill gravy and the big cathead biscuits. Mama made these by rolling biscuit dough into balls with her hands when she lacked the time to roll the mixture with a rolling pin and cut it with a proper cutter.

The sun peeped over Wolf Hill as Littlejim made his way through the sawdust knee-deep in the trench under the big saw. It was his job as dust doodler to remove the sawdust. The saw, larger in diameter than any man on the Creek was tall, shrieked through a log, inches above the top of Littlejim's head. He filled his flat shovel with sawdust. Heaving the shovel, he flung the fragrant wood meal and curly shavings into the wheelbarrow.

When the wheelbarrow was filled, he strained his skinny legs to push it up the incline behind the saw. At the edge of the mill yard, over by the stacks of lumber ready for market, he dumped the load of wood trash on the side of a pile of sawdust that was already higher than a man's head.

"Next week, I'll let you help Fayette load the wagons, if you do a good job today. Then you can haul it to the mine pit up the creek," said Uncle Bob at the start of the work day. Fayette—the men on the Creek called him "Fate"—was the man-of-all-work at the sawmill. He did the odd jobs no one else had time to do. Folks said his mind was slow, but Littlejim thought his quick smile and warm good humor made up for the slowness of mind the Creek folk saw in the gentle little man.

"Clean mill yard is good for business," Uncle Bob said. Bigjim snorted a laugh every time his half-brother said that.

Littlejim knew that Bigjim and Uncle Bob were half-brothers because they had the same father, but different mothers. Uncle Bob's mother had died, and Grandfather had married Miz Caroline, Bigjim's mother. Littlejim also knew that two men could hardly be less alike. Bob was a fat, round man with a bald head, who talked most of the time and laughed a lot. Bigjim was a tall, lean man who seldom laughed and who talked only rarely.

Littlejim had decided that he liked his work as a dust doodler. He liked it especially when Uncle Bob included Littlejim when he addressed the crew as "men." Besides the shiny dime Uncle Bob would give him at the end of the day, he liked working alone. As the big saw whined above his head, he could think his own thoughts. Today, as he carried shovelfuls of sawdust up the incline and threw them into the wagon, he thought about the ideas he had for the essay he would write for the competition. He knew he could never convince his papa to let him enter. But as he worked, he became more convinced in his mind that he would have to risk Papa's disapproval.

As he finished loading the wagon, Uncle Bob blew the whistle on the side of the mill to say it was noon, time for dinner. Mama had packed Littlejim's dinner in a shiny lard can with a red label on the front that said, "Arbuckle Premium Quality Lard."

Uncle Bob and Andy's papa, Mr. McGuire, who

was the head gaffer, came to sit with Littlejim on the bank of the creek. McGuire was a small wiry man who moved constantly. He reminded Littlejim of a small brown bird. Uncle Bob said that Adam McGuire was the lightest man on his feet he had ever seen. That's why he was the head gaffer. He could dance from log to log in the waters of the creek without losing his balance. His was the most highly respected job at the mill yard.

"Air ye being my boy Andy's friend at the school?" asked Mr. McGuire. He used the same strange pronunciations Littlejim had heard at the store.

"Andy a pupil at Osk's blab school up the Creek?" interrupted Uncle Bob.

"Yes," said Mr. McGuire. "You were at Burleson's Store last week, I believe?"

"Yes, sir," said Littlejim. He had never eaten dinner with the head gaffer before. That was quite an honor.

"Littlejim's a pupil at the school, and a mighty good one, too. Right, son?" Uncle Bob always made Littlejim feel proud to be his nephew.

"Well, I try my best, sir," Littlejim said. He blushed.

"Andy ain't bein' much of a scholar, but he's a good boy," said the man, between swipes of his biscuit through the white sawmill gravy in his tin

70

plate. "Says he wants to be a gaffer like me. He won't be needing much schoolin' fer that. But I would like him to git further than I did. No chance for schoolin' in the old country." He pronounced *old* as if it had two syllables—au-old.

Littlejim didn't want to appear rude, but he was curious. "Where is the old country, sir?" he asked, chewing on his ham biscuit.

"Come over from Erin. Ireland, you call it," said Mr. McGuire. "Come to work on the railroads. Helped build the tunnels through the mountains to Asheville, then met Bob here in a sawmilling camp over on the French Broad. He hired me, taught me how to be a gaffer. That's how I come to live here on the Creek."

Littlejim laughed. He tried to imagine short, round Uncle Bob dancing on the logs as they entered the flume. Being a gaffer was the toughest job in the sawmill. It was also the most dangerous. It took a man who could move quickly and lightly on his feet. He watched Mr. McGuire and wondered if his papa didn't realize that Mr. McGuire was the smallest man at the sawmill, yet he had the toughest, most dangerous job. Papa seemed to think that a man's size and strength were the things that made him a man. Mr. McGuire was living proof that size and strength did not make a man important or respected. That

71

was a new thought for the boy. Littlejim would have to think about that some more, he guessed.

"Like a drink of spring water, son?" asked Mr. McGuire. He handed Littlejim his tin watercup.

"Much obliged," said Littlejim. The water tasted good after the salty ham.

"Yes," Mr. McGuire continued, "this land's been mighty good to me. I come here with nothing in my pockets. Now I have land, a home and a fine family. In the old country, I would still be digging peat for pennies a day. Yes, this is a fine land. A good land."

"I reckon most of us come here from sommers else," said Waits Wiseman, who ran the big saw. "I mind my pap telling me about Old Will Wiseman, a-hiding in a tobaccy hogshead on a ship from England. He come here without a penny, too. Served indentureship to pay his passage. He was my great-great-grandfather."

Littlejim was listening intently. He knew Mama's family had come from Germany, but he had always thought of everyone else on the Creek as just being from the Creek.

"Where did Papa's family come from?" Littlejim asked Uncle Bob.

"Well, the Houstons were run out of Scotland, I believe," laughed Uncle Bob. "They fought on the wrong side of the war. As I remember, we fought for

72

the Bonnie Prince Charlie. When he lost, that was worse than being a horse thief. If they had stayed, most of them would have been hanged. So they came to this country and finally found their way to the Creek. We made it here in time to join the Mountain men and fight the British at King's Mountain." Uncle Bob was really into his story. Littlejim thought he might talk all afternoon.

But the men all laughed. "Ain't changed much, have you, Bob?" one of the mill hands said. "Still a family of horse thieves!"

Littlejim opened his mouth to defend Uncle Bob, but his uncle laughed and turned to the man. "Well, at least I ain't been run off from Cane Creek yet, like some as I could name."

Everyone laughed again. Littlejim didn't understand the joke, but he knew that Cane Creek was the next village over the mountain and he had heard that one of the mill hands was courting a young lady in that community.

"I guess most of the Creek folk have been here a-while?" asked Mr. McGuire. "I am the only late newcomer?"

"No, Miz Gertrude, Littlejim's ma, come here as a little girl. Prettiest little girl I ever did see," said Uncle Bob. "I guess all of us are about like the rest of the country. Come here from sommers else."

73

"Come here to find a new life," said Mr. McGuire. "It's a good land, Bob, a good land. I'm mighty proud to be a part of it and have my little ones grow up here." The man's eyes filled with tears.

Uncle Bob smiled at Mr. McGuire.

"We're glad to make you part of us," said Uncle Bob.

"And I hope when my time comes, you'll lay my old bones to rest in this good land. For I'm a part of ye now."

Chapter Eleven

Back and forth. Back and forth. Littlejim pushed one load of wood trash after another to the ever growing dump.

By midafternoon he was so tired his arms felt like they were made of sawdust. He sat on the morning's stack of boards to watch the gaffers as they guided the huge logs through the sluice and lined them up with the edge of the big saw.

"I reckon we all come here from sommers else," the words of Uncle Bob kept ringing in his ears. Maybe that's what it means to be an American. Everybody came here from somewhere else and made this country and this valley their home. He looked up at the Creek Road, following the contour of the creek that had created the little valley, so narrow in places that it was only wide enough for the creek and the road. The mountains loomed on all sides as the shadows of the twin peaks of the Spear Tops made their dark outline on the dancing rays of the winter sun. The big wheel, powered by water flowing through another sluice, turned slowly as the creek poured over the wheel's edge, splashing a waterfall below.

Mr. McGuire was guiding an enormous log into the run. He waved at Littlejim. The tired boy lifted his hand to wave back. As Mr. McGuire stuck the sharp point of the gaff into the bark of the log, he turned. But the log rolled over, and Mr. McGuire's feet flew into the air as he shrieked. Littlejim screamed a warning, but it was useless. Slowly, as if in one of Littlejim's dreams, Mr. McGuire was thrown high into the air. He fell into the narrow stream of the sluice and was pushed down the sluice by the huge log at his feet. For a long moment, Littlejim stood frozen in time.

Littlejim screamed and ran toward the big saw. He reached the man's body just as Uncle Bob stopped the saw. The saw had torn through Mr. McGuire. Littlejim stared in horror at the bloody pieces of the man.

The earth seemed to move in waves beneath Littlejim's feet. He could hardly breathe. He gasped for air.

"But he can't be dead. He just waved at me a minute ago," the boy told Uncle Bob as he caught his

nephew by the shoulder. The boy wrenched away, turned and ran into the bushes that grew along the creek.

Littlejim ran sobbing along the creek bank until he fell. Suddenly he threw up. He picked himself up and ran until his foot caught in a root. He plunged head-first into the mud at the edge of the creek and lay in the edge of the water.

Littlejim looked up. Bigjim was standing there.

"Are you hurt?" his father asked abruptly and turned to walk away. His beard jutted forward reflecting the cold light in his dark eyes, but his hands were shaking. He moved to hide the shaking from his son.

"Papa," Littlejim sobbed. "He was split in two. He was . . ."

Bigjim turned back to face his son. "He was *careless*. Cost him his life," said Bigjim. "Could just as leave happen to you. You be more careful of that saw." And his father was gone into the laurel thicket.

For a long time, Littlejim sat in the mud. He thought of his friend, Andy, who wanted to be a gaffer like his pa. Then he remembered the time Bigjim had chided his son about finding excuses not to go hunting with him.

"Maybe Papa's right," sobbed Littlejim. "Maybe I'm not much of a man." He saw a pair of feet and looked up to see Uncle Bob standing there. He knelt to help Littlejim get up from the mud.

Uncle Bob's warm hand felt good on Littlejim's neck and ear.

"Being a man has nothing to do with it. You've had a hard blow this day, to be sure. We all have. Adam was a good man and a friend. But you're a strong fellow. You'll be all right. You're my nephew," said Uncle Bob. He hugged Littlejim to his big chest, mud and all.

"Poor Andy," sobbed Littlejim. "His papa . . ."

Uncle Bob patted Littlejim's back to comfort him.

"Yes, indeed. A hard blow," said Uncle Bob.

Littlejim sat in Uncle Bob's little office shack and watched out the open door as the crew made a platform of newly sawn boards on one of the pole wagons, loaded Mr. McGuire's body onto the boards and covered it with a blanket.

Uncle Bob reached up above his head and brought a bottle from its hiding place. "Drink this, Jimmy," said Uncle Bob's voice through the fog inside Littlejim's head. Something sweet touched his tongue and burned his stomach as he swallowed it. He managed to open his eyes as he sputtered the strange liquid. He looked up. Uncle Bob took a long drink from a brown bottle and then slipped it into a small space between the rafter and the tin roof.

"Peach brandy," said Uncle Bob with a wink, but his face was very white and his hands shook. "Good for what ails you. Don't let anyone know where my stash is."

"I won't, sir," said Littlejim weakly.

"Come on, we'll take one of the horses and get you home," said his uncle.

Littlejim leaned his head against Uncle Bob's rough coat as the horse trotted down the Creek Road. The smell of Uncle Bob's pipe tobacco and newly sawn wood made Littlejim feel better as he leaned against the man's back. The plodding of the horse and the rough cloth helped Littlejim to know that the world was still real, that he was not lost in some awful dream.

Mama made a fresh pot of coffee while Littlejim sat beside the wood stove trying to get warm. He had never been so cold. Mama mixed milk and sugar into the black liquid and handed a steaming mug to Littlejim and one to Uncle Bob. The first sip burned his tongue.

"Drink up, Jimmy," said Uncle Bob, sipping from his own mug. They drank in silence while Mama peeled potatoes and shredded cabbage for dinner.

Uncle Bob drained his cup. "That was a godsend," he said. "Thanks, Gertrude. So long, Jimmy."

"You'll be back for supper?" Mama asked.

"As soon as me and Jim pay our respects to Miz McGuire," he said. "I'll come back by. Been a hard day."

Mama stood on tiptoe to hug her brother-in-law.

"Thank you, little sister," Uncle Bob said, hugging her. He closed the door softly.

Mama placed the potatoes into a kettle to boil and turned to Littlejim. "Would you like to tell me about it, Jimmy?" she asked quietly.

No words formed in Littlejim's mind. Mama continued to work quietly. The clock in the front room ticked slowly. The fire crackled as the wood in the firebox of the cookstove broke apart.

"Mr. McGuire waved at me," Littlejim said at last.

Mama nodded. "Yes, Jimmy," she said.

"He came to this land with nothing. That was all I could think of."

There was a long silence before Littlejim said anything else.

"Mama, he came here all the way across the ocean from Ireland. This is a good land, he told us at noonday dinner today. He was so glad to be an American . . ." the words came faster and faster. And in a torrent Littlejim told Mama all about Mr. McGuire and the accident and Papa finding him on the creek bank and Uncle Bob bringing him home and all his feelings of the day.

Nell carried Baby May into the kitchen. Mama helped fasten the baby into the highchair and gave each of them a slice of raw potato to chew. Littlejim talked on.

Nell sat by Littlejim on his chair and placed a small arm around her big brother's neck. She patted his back.

Mama left the room. When she returned, she placed a pencil and tablet on the table in front of him, but Littlejim continued to sit as if frozen, staring at the glowing cookstove. His mind would not form words, it would only form pictures of Mr. McGuire's death.

"It has been a hard day, my son," said Mama. "Maybe it will help to put some of it on paper."

Littlejim picked up his pencil and wrote, "Adam McGuire was killed today. He was a good man and he was proud to be an American . . ."

The boy wrote on paper all the words he had told Mama. As he wrote, new words seemed to come from his mind. His fingers flew until they were tired. Then he felt empty. All the jumble of feelings inside him were somehow gone.

"I'm so tired, Mama," he said at last.

"Why don't you lie on our bed in the front room and rest until supper is ready? Nell will stoke the fire so the room will be warm, won't you, Nell?" said Mama.

Littlejim watched the flames dance in the fireplace as he drifted off to sleep.

"I hope when my time comes, you'll lay my old bones to rest in this good land . . ." Mr. McGuire's words echoed over and over inside Littlejim's head. "I'm a part of ye now."

Chapter Twelve

The Saturday following Mr. McGuire's funeral was butchering day. Nell and Littlejim carried load after load of long firewood, and banked it underneath Mama's big black iron wash pots hanging from poles suspended between the two sarvice trees in the barnyard.

By nightfall on Friday, Bigjim and Cousin Tarp had readied the hanging bar, the iron meat hooks and the carving table at the back of the smokehouse. Bigjim had sharpened all of Gertrude's knives on the big round whetstone in the woodshed. He spat on his hand and rubbed the skin of his thumb along the edge of the blade to test its sharpness. Tarp nodded in agreement. Littlejim was allowed to arrange the knives on the carving table set up under the leafless form of the Winter John apple tree for the big day ahead.

Long before the winter sun crept over the top of Wolf Hill that morning, Littlejim had finished his cathead biscuit, slice of sidemeat and gravy. The year past, Littlejim had helped to carry the meat to the kitchen and had worked with the women. This year he was older, and so he would be allowed to work with the men. But as much as he had been looking forward to today, he wished it hadn't come so soon. He still felt light-headed every time he remembered Mr. McGuire. Still, he didn't want to let Papa down, so he didn't ask to work inside.

Nell was to work in the kitchen. Covered with huge aprons, she, Mama and Aunt Josey would work up the meat, making sousemeat from the hogs' heads cooked until the meat fell off the bones. Then they would mix the meat with sage, salt and pepper, and run it through the grinder. The mixture would be placed in the springhouse to jell. The sousemeat would make a fine supper later in the week, served with boiled cabbage and cornbread.

Later, the women would make liver mush from the boiled liver, mixed with cornmeal and gelatin from the bones of the feet and head. When it had jelled, Mama would store it in a crock in the springhouse to fry in slices for breakfast.

But best of all, or so Littlejim thought, was the sausage they would grind and mix with spices. All

85

day long they would cook the batches of sausage on Mama's cookstove to can in glass jars. Littlejim knew that Mama had already made an extra pan of biscuits and that for both dinner and supper that day there would be fresh sausage biscuits. The thought made his mouth water. Sausage was one of his favorite foods.

Littlejim, his father and Cousin Tarp walked out into the frosty morning air. One of the men who worked with Bigjim in the woods already had the fires started. The flames leaped under the iron kettles already filled with water from which steam had begun to rise.

Banjer Brown, from up the head of the Creek, was there to help, puffing on his corncob pipe. He was known to be the best at butchering for miles around and had been there since long before sunup.

Bigjim carried his rifle. The man of the house always did the killing on butchering day. That was his right. As the men approached the hog pen, all the hogs shoved one another for a place close to the fence, waiting for food to be thrown into the trough.

Bigjim stepped one booted foot on the lowest rail of the fence and placed the stock of the rifle against his shoulder. Lowering the barrel to within inches of the shoat's head, he pulled the trigger.

Littlejim's ears heard a cracking sound. The shoat

screamed and fell on his side, one leg still kicking. The other hogs squealed and ran frantically around the pen.

Bigjim took aim again. Another hog lay in the mud of the pen. Banjer Brown leaped over the fence and quickly stabbed each hog's neck with a butcher knife to bleed it as soon as it stopped moving.

Lilac and the other hogs stood in the far corner of the pen, making small rumbling sounds in their throats. Bigjim walked around the corner of the pen, brought an ear of corn out of his coat pocket and offered it to Lilac.

"Open the gate," shouted Bigjim.

The two men dragged the hogs, one after the other, out onto the brown frost-bitten grass. Banjer Brown carried the buckets of boiling water to pour over the hogs' bodies. With sharp butcher knives, Littlejim and Cousin Tarp scraped the bristles quickly from the hide of the first hog and moved on to the second one.

Banjer Brown split the skin of the hogs' hind feet to expose the tendons. Running a gamblin stick, sharpened at each end, through the tendons allowed the hog to be suspended from the supporting pole.

Bigjim and Banjer Brown lifted the pole into a notch between two water oak trees. When Tarp and

Littlejim had cleaned the second hog, the two older men hoisted the hog up beside the first.

Banjer Brown took the largest butcher knife from the cutting table, as Tarp placed a galvanized bucket in front of each of the hanging hogs. With one swift movement, Bigjim slashed the hog down the underbelly. With a second cut the intestines oozed into the buckets, steaming in the cold air.

The sweet stench of blood and hog guts hit Littlejim's stomach like a blow from a fist to his middle. The bloody body of the head gaffer at Uncle Bob's sawmill appeared before his eyes just as he had seen it last week. The world swam in and out so he could not see clearly. He dropped the bloody knife he was holding and ran for the outhouse door.

"No-account boy . . ." he heard Bigjim say, as his stomach exploded into his mouth.

Mama came to the outhouse door with a cool wet cloth. She washed Littlejim's face and helped him walk back to the house.

"It is my opinion," said Mama, standing firmly with a fist on each hip facing her tall husband and daring him to disagree, "that my son has the terrible influenza that is going around. He should stay in bed this day."

So while the rest of the family worked to prepare the winter store of meat, Littlejim lay, a lump of misery, in his bed in the sleeping loft. He wanted to go back outside but everytime he went to get up, the picture of Mr. McGuire flashed in his head and he lay back down.

"I wish," he said to the ceiling, "that I was dead. I hate you, Papa." But he dared not think such a sinful thought. No wonder Bigjim thought he was a no-account boy.

Chapter Thirteen

Early February brought sunny days. The cold weather was not yet behind them for the year, but with the melting snows a stirring of green wisps showed on the sunny banks facing the creek as here and there a crocus lifted its face to the warmth.

"Time to turn the sod to make ready for planting," Bigjim said to his son as they forked hay down from the haystack in the bottom land across the creek from the Houston home. "Think you can handle the hillside plow this year?"

Littlejim beamed and threw a great forkful of hay on top of Old Jerse, the cow. The brown and white head slowly and methodically shook off the hay and kept on chewing.

"Yes, sir. I think I can," the boy answered. If his papa thought he could handle the big two-horse hillside plow for turning the sod on the garden plot, high up the steep side of the hill, then he surely must believe his son ready to take on a man's duties, or so his son thought.

"If you can handle the plowing, I'll take time from the woods to do the harrowing. Maybe I can get Banjer to lay off the rows. Borrow some horses from Bob, mayhap we can get the crops in by Good Friday," said Bigjim.

"I'll do my best, Papa," said Littlejim proudly. He wondered why the crops had to be in by Good Friday. Last year Good Friday was early in March. This year it would be late April, but all the people on the Creek who planted by the signs believed their crops must be planted no later than Good Friday. Papa's voice interrupted his thoughts.

"Well, it ain't as if you're much of a man," said his father, jumping down from the haystack and striding across the brown stubble of the meadow. Littlejim jumped down and ran to catch up with his father's long legs. He fell into step. His father only walked faster. Littlejim stumbled trying to keep up with the tall man. The sun was sinking and the sky grew darker.

"What did you say, Papa?" asked Littlejim.

"I said it ain't as if you're much of a man," Bigjim stopped and glared down at his son, his mouth a straight line beneath the mustache. Littlejim shrank

91

and turned away. "Acting like a sickly calf at the butchering last week and all. But you're about the best to be had on this farm right now. So I guess you'll have to do."

The man turned abruptly and walked away.

"Go on to the house," he called over his shoulder.

Littlejim walked slowly toward the kitchen door. He could see Mama's head through the window silhouetted against the lamplight. He began to run toward the light.

A horse was tied to the apple tree in the front yard. Cousin Tarp stepped down from the stirrups. He carried a bag slung over his shoulder. Nell and her friend, Emma, came running around from the side yard. She ran up to hug Cousin Tarp. He picked up both girls and carried them toward the house.

"Howdy, Littlejim," he said. "You're in a mighty big hurry. I thought Bigjim might like some tobaccer seedlings." He set the girls on the ground and they ran up the front steps into the house. Cousin Tarp thrust the bag toward Littlejim.

"I'm sure he'd be pleased," said the boy. "Mama will want to see you. Come on in."

The door opened and Mama stood waiting with her arms outstretched.

"Tarp, you are a sight for sore eyes," she said. "Do come in."

"Howdy, Gertrude," said Tarp. "I stopped by with some tobaccer seedlings for Bigjim. He still in the woods?"

"No, he was tending the stock with Jimmy. Where is your papa?" She turned to her son.

"Last I seen of him he was going toward the Bad Branch," said Tarp. "Headed that way when I rode up. Don't worry him. I'll just leave these seedlings with you," said Tarp.

"Won't you sit a spell and have a cup of coffee?" asked Mama. "I just took a dried-apple pie out of the oven."

"Neva'll have supper on time as I get home. But, Lordy, Gertrude, you could tempt a man away from his supper with your apple pie. It is sure to be the best in the county."

"Tarp Burleson! Words like that will get you two slices of pie," said Mama, blushing. "And I've never seen you turn down pie since I was only a bit of a girl."

Littlejim thought Tarp was mighty lucky to get to have his pie before supper. Mama would never allow any of the family to do that. He knew that Tarp was Mama's favorite of the cousins from Bigjim's family. They had been friends since they were children and walked to school together.

"Bigjim orta be mighty proud. Prettiest wife—

well, maybe Neva's as pretty—and the best cook for sure on the Creek Road. Lordy. Lordy." The scrawny man took off his hat, placed it carefully on the hook by the door and washed his hands.

Mama poured the coffee and sliced a generous piece of pie for her guest. Tarp pulled his chair close to the table and began to eat as if he rarely saw food. Mama smiled and shrugged her shoulders.

"If I didn't know Geneva," said Mama, laughing, "I'd say you hadn't tasted food in at least a week. Always you look like the seven years' famine in Egypt. It is a thin man you are."

"The Lord put good food on earth for man to eat and enjoy," laughed Tarp, between bites of Mama's flaky piecrust. He took a great swallow of coffee and cleaned the last crumb from his plate.

Littlejim watched but his mind was on something else.

"Could you show me how to make a tobacco bed, Cousin Tarp?" he asked at last.

"Mighty glad to show you, son," said Tarp. "You going to make a farmer? I hear tell you orta be a scholar."

"He will be scholar," said Mama. "But he may want to be a farmer, too. What do you have in mind?"

"I thought I could start Papa's tobacco bed for

94

him. And we would not tell him until his tobacco was grown," said Littlejim.

"Why would you do that?" asked Mama, looking at him intently.

"Well, Papa enjoys a chaw and last year he didn't have time to tend the tobacco, so it didn't make. I thought to surprise him this year."

Mama folded her arms across the front of her embroidered apron and smiled at Littlejim.

"And that is what we will do, my little love," she said, kissing her son's hair where it fell over his forehead.

Chapter Fourteen

"Pile the soil all around the boards, Jimmy," said Mama. "We want the tiny plants to be warm."

Littlejim carefully banked the soil around the frames of the three oblong beds Mama had formed near the garden fence. Cousin Tarp had helped the boy spade the soil and rake it until it looked like fine dark powder. By noonday dinner, Tarp had left to work the soil in his own garden.

Littlejim and Mama worked all afternoon sowing the seeds for lettuce and placing the tiny onion sets in holes dug into the soil with their fingers. Among the onions, Mama had sown radish seeds, not bothering to plant them in rows. Radishes would be the first vegetable to mature in the garden and would be picked as soon as they could be eaten. Other vegetables planted with them would have more time and space to grow.

Finally Mama helped Littlejim plant the tiny tobacco plants in a separate bed off in another corner.

"We will let your papa think we have another lettuce bed," winked Mama at Littlejim. "Shall we?"

"I think this will make Papa happy," said Littlejim. "I think tobacco tastes terrible, but most of the men here on the Creek chew it. If I chewed tobacco, do you think Papa would think I was a man?"

"Jimmy!" said Mama. "Chewing tobacco does not make you a man. You are a scholar. You want to learn to be a gentleman. A gentleman does not rely on tobacco to prove himself."

"Isn't Papa a gentleman?" asked her son.

His mother stood looking into the distance for a long moment before she answered. "Your papa is a fine man, in his own way," she said. "He is a good man. He did not have a chance to learn the ways of a gentleman. That does not make him less of a man. But you, my son, will have the chance your papa did not have, *if* you do not take up chewing tobacco!"

Mama's eyebrows were raised, and Littlejim knew that whether Bigjim chewed tobacco or not made little difference. But he knew that if her son chewed tobacco, Mama would be very disappointed in him. And he did not want to disappoint her.

Mama stretched canvas around the edge of the board frame and Littlejim drove in the nails to hold it in place. The canvas would provide a warm bed where the tiny seeds and plants could mature protected from the winter winds still to blow down from the Spear Tops.

"Mama, I've been thinking about the essay competition," Littlejim said. "You know the day Mr. McGuire was killed when I wrote and wrote on my tablet."

"Yah," his mother said. "And putting what happened into words helped you to feel better, did it not?"

"Yes, and I keep remembering what Mr. McGuire said that day, Mama. He said, 'I hope when my time comes, you'll lay my old bones to rest in this good land. For I'm a part of ye now.' I think what he was saying was that he felt he was an American, not an Irishman. So that is one thing it means to be an American."

"My fine son, I think you are right. My fadde always said he felt he was an American when he found he was counting in English instead of German," Mama chuckled.

"And Mr. Wiseman told a story about his grandfather who stowed away on a ship to be an American," Littlejim said. "It seems that being an American means something different to everybody. How can I write about all those different meanings?"

"Ah, perhaps, my son, what all those meanings mean is that every person has found a place where he belongs, where he is an American. What do you think, my Jimmy?" she asked, looking intently into her son's eyes. Her son thought about the words she had spoken.

"Every person has found a place where he belongs," repeated Littlejim. His eyes brightened and he smiled at her.

"That's it. I think that's what they mean, too, Mama, but I don't know how to put it into words," said Littlejim.

"We are finished here," said Mama. "Put the tools away. There is still time before dark for writing on a fine young man's essay."

Littlejim gathered the tools to return them to the woodshed. Mama returned to the house to her sewing.

Littlejim climbed the narrow stairs to his room. He took out his tablet and pencil. For a long time he sat staring at the tree outside his window as the March wind blew the branches back and forth.

"What it means to be an American," he wrote. He chewed on his pencil and thought about his essay.

He wrote, "I knew a man named Adam McGuire. He was the head gaffer in my Uncle Bob's sawmill on Henson Creek. He had a good house and a family.

Being a gaffer is hard work, but he always had a pleasant word and a smile for everybody. The other people who lived on the Creek respected Mr. McGuire.

"One day he told me that this country had been good to him. He had come from Ireland to work on the railroads here. He said if he had not come to America, he would be shoveling peat for pennies a day, but at Uncle Bob's sawmill he made almost fifty cents a day. That is a good wage, so Mr. McGuire earned a good living.

"On the day he died, he said this country had been good to him and that he wanted his bones to rest in American soil. Adam McGuire was happy to be an American even if he came from somewhere else. So I guess that's what it means to be an American."

Littlejim chewed on his pencil some more. Then he stared out the window.

"Jimmy! Jimmy!" Mama's voice was far away, but it sounded as if something terrible had happened.

"Jimmy, come help me! Lilac's out of the pen!"

Littlejim quickly hid his pencil and tablet away. He ran down the stairs, through the kitchen and out the back door.

Mama was standing in the garden flapping her apron at Lilac, the huge sow. Lilac had already torn the canvas on the tobacco bed and was standing near one side of the frame. She was rooting her nose into the canvas and the soil beneath it. Tiny tobacco plants came flying from beneath her front feet.

"Mama! Papa's tobacco bed!" cried Littlejim, running toward Lilac.

Mama had grabbed a hoe and was hitting Lilac's back with little effect on the pig. Lilac continued her rooting.

Littlejim ran to the corncrib, opened the door and grabbed two ears of corn. Quickly he shucked the husks from the ears and ran toward Lilac.

"Sooey, Lilac, sooey," he called. He waved the ears of corn toward the pig's face. Finally, Lilac sniffed the air and trotted toward Littlejim. He threw one of the ears on the ground. Lilac stopped to munch. He reached down and grabbed the corn. Then he began to run toward the pigpen. Mama followed with her hoe prodding Lilac's backside.

Littlejim led Lilac back into the pen while Mama guarded the opening. Then he brought the hammer and nails to repair the rails. Mama helped him to secure the fence, then she said, "The tobacco bed is ruined, Jimmy. We'll have to start all over."

"I wanted to grow Papa's tobacco. I wanted to show Papa I could do something he cared about, but Lilac ruined the bed," said Littlejim sadly.

101

"You will show your papa, tobacco bed or no to-bacco bed, my son," she said. "But right now, we start again. I will cut some more canvas, and you will go to Tarp's and get some more plants. We do not give up! Lilac or no Lilac!"

When Mama said "Ve do not gif up!" her son knew that she could do anything. He set out across the hill to Tarp's house for more tobacco plants. They would start all over.

"We will start all over," Mama had said.

"That's what Mr. McGuire did when he came from Ireland," thought Littlejim as he walked through the dusk. "And Opa and Oma, too." He smiled at the thought of Opa suddenly counting in English. "And old Will Wiseman and all the others. They started over. I can start over, too."

The thought gave new energy to Littlejim's steps as he crossed the footlog to Tarp's house.

Chapter Fifteen

Dust clouds covered the figures in the garden plot on the sunny slope above Bigjim's house. The clay and rich brown soil was dry so it fogged as the workers prepared it for planting.

By midmorning, Littlejim was near the lower edge of the cornfield. He had the reins draped around his shoulders as he struggled to control the big plow dragging into the earth behind Scott and Swain. As he reached the end of the cleared area, he stopped the horses and walked around to the moldboard. Opening a latch, he turned the moldboard so the soil would be turned in the opposite direction as the horses again crossed the land.

Farther up the slope Bigjim wrestled with the wooden harrow, its metal stakes tearing the earth and smoothing it behind the horses' hooves. Finally, near the highest point of the slope, Banjer Brown followed the horse pulling a single-foot layoff plow which laid off the soil into neat straight rows.

Littlejim reached the lower edge of the cornfield and stopped the horses. Despite the chill wind that blew down from the ridge, his face was wet. He slipped the horses out of their traces and pulled the plow over to the shade of a tree.

Mama and Nell trudged up the hill carrying water jugs, two bags of corn and several hoes. Littlejim took one of the hoes and the bag of corn from Mama. They walked to the top of the slope.

"Ready for planting, Jimmy?" Mama asked with a smile.

"Papa hasn't found anything wrong with the plowing yet," said Littlejim.

"That is good," said Mama. She walked over to Bigjim and lifted the water jug. He stopped the horses and took a long drink. Then he wiped his mouth on his sleeve and called, "Giddiup."

Mama offered Littlejim a drink of water, then she met Banjer Brown at the end of his row to share with him.

At the top of the slope, Mama slung the bag of corn over her shoulder and began to drop the grains of corn into the row. She dropped two grains, then took a step. Two grains more and took a step. Nell followed, covering the corn with a thin layer of soil.

Soon Bigjim picked up a bag of corn and joined his family. Without a word, Littlejim began to cover the corn his father had dropped.

"Tarp's coming to cover for Banjer," said Bigjim finally. "With him, we ought to be done by dinnertime. Have to get this corn in the ground. It's Good Friday. Corn has to be planted no later than Good Friday or it won't have time to ripen before first frost."

Nell asked, "Why does Mr. Osk always say that corn must be planted by Good Friday even if Good Friday comes on Sunday?" She looked puzzled.

"Because Good Friday can't come on Sunday, Nell," laughed her brother. "He's making fun. Good Friday can only be on Friday."

"Oh," said Nell, laughing.

Bigjim ignored their mirth. "The signs are in the heart next week. Plant then and the corn will make small ears," he said.

"What does Papa mean, the signs are in the heart, Mama?" asked Nell.

"Your papa believes in the signs from the stars written in the almanac," said Mama. "I planted the cucumbers last week when the signs were in Gemini, the twins. Most people on the Creek plant by the signs."

"I don't understand," said Nell.

"The sun and stars make certain signs in the sky," said Bigjim. "These are signs from God about planting and harvesting. Signs were used in the Bible, so's we ought to keep using them. We plant corn today because it's an old moon. That will keep the corn from growing too tall and making small ears."

Littlejim stared at his father's back. He had seldom heard Bigjim talk for such a long time. His father must think the signs were important to talk so long about them.

"Dinner's made this day," said Mama. "It's in a basket at the spring by the horses."

"Then we'll finish after noontime dinner," said Bigjim, pointing to the lower rows.

"I want to plant some pole beans along with the last few rows of corn," said Mama.

Littlejim knew that most of the Creek folks planted their beans and corn together so the beans could climb the cornstalks for support. That way two crops could be tended at the same time. By the time the corn was ready, the beans had been harvested and most of the vines were dried up. But by planting them together, two crops were cultivated at the same time and the land grew twice as much food.

Finally, they stopped work and the family washed up in the stream for dinner. Bigjim started a fire and Mama filled the coffeepot. She set it on the fire to boil and placed a skillet on a rock at the edge of the flame. Lifting sliced bacon from a bowl, she placed it in the skillet. Soon it began to sizzle.

Littlejim warmed his back by the fire. The March wind still held a chill in it. The fragrance of bacon and coffee teased Littlejim's tongue, and his mouth began to water.

Mama lifted a bowl from the basket. Inside it were buttered wedges of cornbread. Then she brought out a towel in which were wrapped the first of her spring onions. Finally she unwrapped a towel in which were wrapped some tiny dark green leaves. Bigjim stopped stirring sugar into his coffee to look.

"Branch lettuce!" he said, a smile widening his mustache. "Where did you get branch lettuce?"

"First of the spring," said Mama. "Nell found it growing at the edge of the Bad Branch yesterday. She picked it this morning for our noonday dinner."

Mama chopped the spring onions and tore the branch lettuce into bite-sized pieces and placed them in a large bowl. When the bacon was crisp, she tore it into tiny pieces and sprinkled it on top of the lettuce and onions. Then she poured the hot fat over the mixture. Littlejim could hear the sizzle as the lettuce was wilted. Mama stirred and then divided the delicacy on the plates she had brought.

She placed the bounty on a colored cloth. When

107

Littlejim and Nell had filled their cups half full of coffee, Mama poured milk from a pitcher to the tops. The hot liquid warmed Littlejim from the chill wind.

"Branch lettuce marks the spring. Warm days are ahead," said Banjer Brown. "First I've seed this year."

Littlejim almost said, "It's seen, not *seed*," then he remembered his manners. Mama said that even if you knew better, it was not seemly to correct folks.

"One of nature's best bounties," agreed Mama. "To give us such good greens when the snow is barely past should make us think of spring. It is so good to taste something green after the long winter!"

"Fine goods," was all Bigjim could say, sopping the last morsel with his buttered cornbread. "If the weather holds, we should have 'ros' nears' by July Fourth," said Bigjim.

Almost no one on the Creek roasted the ears of corn. Everyone boiled them in a big black kettle over an open fire. But fresh corn on the cob was still called "ros' nears" by everyone Littlejim knew.

"Just in time for the dinner on the ground on Grassy Ridge Bald," said Mama, smiling at her husband.

"Now, Gert. We always go to the singing and the dinner on the ground," said Bigjim. "But I don't want to hear anymore about my son a-speaking there." He took a big bite from his chunk of cornbread.

Littlejim looked at Mama and took a sip of coffee to soothe the lump in his throat.

"We shall have corn for the July Fourth dinner on the ground," said Mama smiling. "Other things will follow."

Mama winked at her son and reached into her apron pocket. She brought out a cloth tied in a small bundle.

"Have a sweet cake, James," she said.

Littlejim smiled. A sweet cake would tempt his father to kindness when nothing else would.

The boy lay back under the pine tree and thought about the July Fourth dinner on the ground. He could almost taste the buttery kernels of "ros' nears" as he thought about them.

"Maybe I'll eat some of this corn on the day I read my essay," he thought. "Maybe that's what I'll do that day."

He remembered how angry Papa had been when they talked at the dinner table. But he decided he had to send his essay to the competition, no matter what Papa said. If his words did not make it to be printed in the *Star,* he would just have to face his papa's anger.

Ever since the day Adam McGuire was killed at the sawmill, Littlejim had been thinking about what the man had said about coming to a new country to make his home. That part was written already. Maybe finding a place where you belonged, like Mama said, was what it meant to be an American. He would just have to think on it some more.

"Woolgathering again?" barked Bigjim, startling his son out of his thoughts. "Time to get to work if we're going to get this corn planted by sundown."

"Yes, sir," answered Littlejim quickly.

Chapter Sixteen

"Jimmy. Jimmy, my little love, wake up."

Mama's voice sounded through the fog of sleep inside Littlejim's head. It was too cold. He didn't want to wake up. The small window at the end of the sleeping loft was dark. Only a sliver of moon shone through the branches of the chestnut tree outside.

"Jimmy, your father needs you to drive the second wagon along with him to Spruce Pine today," Mama's voice said.

"Today is school," mumbled Littlejim. Mama did not like for her children to miss a day when school was in session.

"Hurry, love. This shipment must go out to the army today. Robert cannot leave. There's no one else," said Mama.

She helped Littlejim to sit up. She kissed his hair,

and placed one of his arms into the sleeve of the warm flannel shirt hanging on the chair by his bed.

"I can do it, Mama." Littlejim pulled away. He was not a baby who had to be dressed.

"So you can. I'll have you some breakfast ready when you come down to the kitchen. Hurry, now."

She left the kerosene lamp on the floor by the top of the stairs.

Although it was late April, Littlejim shivered from the cold. He buttoned up the back flap of his long woolen underwear and climbed into his pants. His stiff fingers managed to tie the laces of his heavy winter boots. He pulled on his heavy sweater, added his warm coat and pulled his toboggan cap over his ears. He grabbed his mittens and picked up the lamp. Halfway down the narrow stairs, he ran back to the bed. Under his pillow he had hidden some precious pages which he had worked on late into the night. He stuffed them into his shirt pocket.

When he got to Mama's warm kitchen, Bigjim and Uncle Bob were there drinking coffee. Littlejim sat down at the table. He lifted the mug of warm sweet coffee to his lips.

"Jimmy. Wash your face and comb your hair before you sit at my table," said Mama.

"Gert, no time for fancies today. We have a load of lumber to deliver," barked Bigjim.

"Now, Jim, let the boy clean up and eat his break-fast. He'll be the better for it," said Uncle Bob, with a wink at his nephew.

Littlejim broke the ice in the washbasin on the back porch to wash his face. Then he combed his hair, all without taking off his coat. Dripping water onto his collar, he sat down at the table. Quickly he ate the hot apple turnover Mama lifted to his plate.

Uncle Bob walked with Littlejim out to where the two wagons sat loaded at the edge of the road. The horses snorted, their breath like twin curls of steam out of Mama's teakettle.

Littlejim had often handled a farm wagon, and oc-casionally Fayette had allowed him to manage a half-empty pole wagon around the mill yard. But as he looked up at the pole wagons fully loaded with lumber, the load looked higher than Spear Tops Mountain. He felt proud that Uncle Bob and his fa-ther thought he was man enough to handle such an important job.

The pole wagon had no box on it like a farm wagon. It was only two sets of wheels joined by a coupling pole. The stack of boards rested front to back on two bolsters built over the front and back axles. The back bolster was braced solid with the axle, but the front axle was attached to the bolster by a wooden pin to allow the axle to turn corners. The boards were fastened down with chains that were wrapped all the way around both the lumber and the coupling pole. The wheels on the wagon were as tall as Littlejim's shoulders and were outlined with metal rims that helped the wagon get through the muddy roads. Brake blocks were attached to each of the thick wooden wheels. The brakes were controlled by a brake lever beside the right front wheel.

As soon as he climbed onto the four boards Uncle Bob's men had placed forward so they stuck out in front of the rest of the load to form a seat, Littlejim checked to make sure his arms could reach the brake lever. Just barely.

"Be sure you can get to the brake lever, Jimmy," said Uncle Bob. "That's the most important part of your job. The horses can do most of the rest of the trip themselves."

Littlejim looked up behind his head. The stack of boards was just a bit taller than he was. The horses would have a hard time with such a heavy load.

Uncle Bob handed him his dinner bucket and a sack of leaves to cushion where he sat. Then Bigjim set two baskets of apples on the seat boards beside the boy and tied them securely with ropes.

"Promised P. D. Price to deliver some of Gert's Winter John apples on this trip, last of the year. Mind you, they're your mama's finest. Don't spill a

114

one. And don't eat more than two samples," said Uncle Bob, as he reached up playfully to pull Littlejim's toboggan cap down over his eyes. He looked at Littlejim's worried face as the boy straightened the cuff of his cap. Then he slapped his nephew on the knee.

"Jimmy, don't you fret. I am trusting you with a man's job. You can do it. This lumber has to go out on the two o'clock train. Remember, son, today the U.S. Army is depending on you. I am, too," his uncle said.

Bigjim slapped the reins on his wagon, just ahead of Littlejim's. His big wagon creaked as the team strained with the load on it.

On the back wagon, Littlejim smacked his lips together and snapped the reins. "Giddiup," he said. Scott and Swain, Bigjim's matched Percherons, set their huge hooves on the roadbed at almost the same time. One side of the wagon lurched forward, then the other. The lumber swayed above Littlejim's head. Then the team began to move in rhythm. Littlejim felt the wagon sway gently side to side in time to the horses' steps. A chill April wind burned the boy's cheeks and nose.

The two wagons met the rising sun of the chilly spring day at the crossroads where the Creek Road met the River Road that led into the town eight miles away. They passed a few wagons and buggies on the River Road. Bigjim tipped his slouch hat, and called a howdy once in a while to a passerby. At Wright's Curve, they met Mr. Vance and Ivor in their buggy. Littlejim waved at the older boy, who waved back and shouted, "Hold the reins, Littlejim."

He felt very much a man as he handled the reins of the team hauling the heavy load. Littlejim was very proud to have his friend see him in charge of the team.

"Uncle Bob had said I am almost a man. Now maybe at last Papa will see I am growing up and will be proud of me, too. I have to be my very best today," he said to Scott and Swain.

"What be ye doing back there, boy?" called Bigjim, leaning around the side of the stack of lumber on the front wagon.

"Nothing, Papa," said Littlejim. "Just talking to myself."

"Fool dreamer," snorted Bigjim. "Always wool-gathering."

The road ran along the course of the North Toe River. Daily use had worn deep ruts that the wagon wheels could follow. Some of the ruts were filled with muddy water that splashed up on Littlejim's shoes. The road and the bank above it were studded with rocks too big for man and horse to move. Some-

116

times the road jogged to miss the largest of those that formed part of the roadbed.

As the wagons approached Davenport Bridge, they paused and Littlejim searched the upper bank for marks left by the picks, shovels and dragpans the local men had used to widen the road. The shipments of goods for the war made a wider road necessary from the farms in Avery County to the rail yard in the neighboring county. Then the two wagons passed the place where he could remember hiding with Uncle Bob around the curve while the blasts of dynamite loosened the soil and rocks so the men and horses could move them from the road.

Littlejim had been too young to help with the work then. But one day, when Papa and Uncle Bob had brought their teams of big timber horses to pull the heavy dragpans, Uncle Bob had brought Littlejim with him to watch. He remembered how Uncle Bob had allowed him to sit on Scott's broad back when the huge horse pulled the flat metal pan heaped to the top of its three sides with soil and rocks. Scott pulled the pan from the upper bank to dump a load off the lower bank toward the river. Back and forth, back and forth, until a firm, almost flat roadbed was made.

Uncle Bob had told Littlejim that each man who hauled goods over the River Road had been con-

117

scripted to give a week's work toward improving the road. By working together the men of the neighboring counties, Avery and Mitchell, built one of the finest roads in the Blue Ridge Mountains of North Carolina, or so said Uncle Bob when he was in a bragging mood.

Littlejim was proud that he had ridden on Scott's big back to help build that road, but Bigjim had only snorted, "Boy's just in the way. No-account young'un."

But Uncle Bob had wound his arms tighter around the boy's ribs where Littlejim sat on the saddle in front of his uncle that day. Bigjim's voice trailed off as he began to hitch the horses to their traces. Littlejim could no longer hear the words, but his eyes still stung with tears.

"Best be on our way if we're to make the two o'clock train," called Bigjim, heaving himself up to the driver's place on the load of lumber.

The morning sun was growing warmer. Littlejim took off his coat, and hung it on the end of one of the boards. The last long climb before they reached Spruce Pine was Riverhill, which began at Davenport Bridge and wound, shaped by the crescent of the river, into the edge of the little railroad town. He giddiupped the horses, and the steep climb up Riverhill began.

Chapter Seventeen

Littlejim had been into town twice in the past, but he had forgotten the bustle of the place. It seemed to him that everybody was in a hurry. He and his father approached the spot where the main road divided into Upper Street, higher up the hill parallel to the river, and Lower Street, lower on the hill parallel to the river. The number of wagons and carriages increased. Here and there, an automobile added its noise to the confusion.

Bigjim pointed his whip to the left. The wagons would follow Lower Street down an incline to the place where the street ran alongside the railroad track beside the river. About halfway down the street stood the railroad station.

The street was muddy, but had a board sidewalk, with parking for buggies and hitching posts for the horses beside it. They drove the wagons slowly past

Spruce Pine Store Company and J. D. Lawing General Merchandise Company and stopped in front of Peterson's Pharmacy.

"Got to deliver these apples," said Bigjim. "You mind these hosses. Bob's team ain't as skittish as Scott and Swain here."

Littlejim climbed up on top of the load of boards. He could see the sign that read "Charles Peterson, Medical Doctor," with an arrow pointing upward to the second story of the building. Next door was the sign for P. D. Price's Provisions Company.

Mr. Price came out the front door of the building wearing a white apron that was stained with blood over his fat stomach. He was carrying a meat cleaver. A boy about the age of Littlejim followed close behind. A tall, stalwart man in a fine gray suit and hat walked with the pair.

"Howdy, Mr. Price," said Bigjim.

"Howdy do, Jim," said Mr. Price. "How be you?"

After Mr. Price had wiped his hands on his apron, the two men shook hands.

"Tolerable well, just tolerable," said Bigjim. "Brought your Winter Johns."

"Fine-looking fruit. Prime quality. Just prime," said Mr. Price.

Littlejim helped the other boy lift the baskets of Winter John apples down to the sidewalk.

The man in the gray suit walked ahead to inspect Uncle Bob's team of Clydesdales. Then he walked back to examine the strong leg muscles of Scott and Swain.

"Come by after you get unloaded. I'll settle up with Miz Houston then. Got a setup for your fine drayman here, too," Mr. Price laughed.

Littlejim hoped the setup would include a choice of a slice of hoop cheese like Mr. Burleson usually gave him. His mouth watered. It was getting past his midday dinnertime, and his stomach had begun to growl.

The tall man walked up to Bigjim and tipped his hat. He flicked the ash off a long cigar.

"Mr. Houston, I'm George G. Green. I own the livery stable here. Do a little horse trading, too. That's as fine a team of Percherons as I've ever laid my eyes on. Good team of Clydesdales, too. Wouldn't like to sell, would you?"

Never before in all his life had Littlejim seen his father smile so broadly that he showed his teeth. But this time Bigjim grinned. His straight, even teeth shone from within his beard in the noonday sun. He rocked back and forth from heel to toe, toe to heel. His thumbs laced his suspenders.

"My pets, Scott and Swain? No, sir! I'd sooner sell that no-account boy there as part with them hosses.

121

They be like part of my life's blood." Littlejim felt proud of Scott and Swain. But his father's words stung. "Of course, the other team's my brother's, so's they ain't fer sale neither," Bigjim continued.

Mr. Green walked over to Littlejim and picked up one arm.

"Open your mouth, son," he said with a broad wink.

Littlejim opened his mouth. Mr. Green pretended to examine the boy's teeth as he had examined the horses' and then slapped him on the back.

"Yep, fine young man you've got there. Wouldn't mind having a son like him myself, but no market these days for boys." He winked at Littlejim again. "Percherons, though, I've got a market for them."

"Mighty good of you to ask," said Bigjim. "But they ain't fer sale. Good day." He tipped his slouch hat and turned back to the wagons.

"If you change your mind, you'll find me at the livery stable next to the Topliff Hotel on Upper Street. Good day to you both," said Mr. Green.

He walked away and disappeared into a side street that ran between Price's Provisions and the building with a sign that read "Bradley Masters, Painless Dentist, Upstairs."

Bigjim pointed to a gray and black building on the left a short distance down the street. It had a sign

122

that read "Clinchfield Railroad" on the side. A huge black locomotive hissed steam near the office entrance. Another engine headed in the other direction waited on the side track nearer the river.

"I'll pull the wagon over there. You head up to Upper Street, to the next side street, and come down and line up at the siding at the other end of the station. Then you'll be heading in the right direction for unloading. I'll see Sam McKinney fer the papers." His father pointed one long skinny finger across the wagon in front of Littlejim.

Littlejim's eyes followed his father's hand as he indicated directions. He nodded his head, trying to follow what the man said.

Bigjim had already pulled his wagon off to the rail yard. Littlejim directed the team to turn up the steep side street to the broad road higher on the hill. He had to wait in line until the wagons in front could move into the flow of traffic on the main street. While he waited, he took the papers on which he had begun his essay out of his pocket. Between moves, he read the lines aloud to hear how his words sounded.

At the intersection, he stopped the team to allow a buggy to pass down the hill. He dropped the reins loosely to his knee. A lone rider on a bay horse streaked by in front of Scott and Swain. The horses stepped back in tandem, skipping the brake blocks away from the wheels of the wagon. The papers with his essay written on them fell into the mud unseen.

At that same moment, the locomotive down the hill behind the wagon released a puff of steam. Its whistle blew. The team lurched forward. Muscles straining in fear, Scott and Swain began to run as fast as their huge feet could move, dragging Littlejim and his wagonload of lumber with them as they turned the corner.

Careening wildly, the team and wagon tore along Upper Street, with Littlejim hanging onto the load of lumber for dear life. He grabbed for the brake lever. Nothing happened. It was loose.

The horses ran on. Dogs, chickens, people and other vehicles scattered. Guests at the Topliff Hotel left their white rocking chairs to stare. Several men ran out of the Post Office to watch. As the wagon passed, some of the men began to laugh and point at the runaways.

Littlejim tried the brakes again, but there were no brakes.

"Why don't some of these men help me?" Littlejim asked the wind as it whizzed by his ears, between cries of "Whoa! Stop!" But everyone just stood on the sidewalk and watched. The team had turned down the side street when Littlejim finally realized

the reins were dangling between the rumps of Scott and Swain. He lay sideways, then turned around so that his body was partly off the load of boards, holding on with one hand. Finally he caught the reins with the other.

Managing to sit up, he pulled on the reins. The horses did not respond. He pulled again, yelling, "Whoa. Whoa. Stop!" The team slowed down, then came to a stop in front of Peterson's Pharmacy, headed in the direction opposite Bigjim's wagon parked nearby.

Littlejim wiped his wet face on his sleeve and climbed up to stand on the boards on legs that wobbled from weak knees.

Just as he caught his breath, the train whistle blew again. The team bolted and away they went. The thrust of the wagon threw Littlejim backward on top of the load of lumber. The reins flew out of his hands, dragging beneath the horses' hooves.

The wagon careened wildly down the street, up the hill and along the sidewalk. The horses began to run first to one side of the street, then to the other. Drivers of other wagons and buggies scurried to safety, but Littlejim's wagon barely missed one parked on Upper Street.

Down the hill the horses ran. Along Lower Street, passing the railroad station, they barely slowed on the turn as they started up the incline.

Littlejim struggled to turn on his side. He saw his papa's slouch hat and dark beard coming out the door of the station as he passed. Up the hill they went again. Littlejim's fear was so big he could not breathe. He could feel the lumber swaying from side to side. He closed his eyes and prayed.

As they passed the livery stable, a tall figure ran out into the street. His fine gray hat flew into the mud. The man leaped to Scott's side, and managed to throw a leg over the horse's back. Then he grabbed Swain's bridle. Mr. George G. Green, owner of the livery stable, pulled the team to a stop. The load of boards jerked and swayed but remained upright.

"Are you all right, son?" the man asked as he jumped down the side of the wagon.

"The brakes were gone. Nobody would help me. Some of them were laughing at me," said Littlejim, between gulps of air. "Thank you, sir."

Mr. Green held his sides and leaned against the muddy wheel of the wagon. He caught his breath at last.

"Son, they were laughing at your coat that hung on this board for your entire wild ride," said the man, handing the coat to Littlejim. Mr. Green laughed then. Littlejim managed a smile. The man stepped up on the wheel, sat down beside Littlejim and guided the wagon into the railroad siding.

Bigjim came loping over to the wagon. "My lord,

son! What do you mean, letting that team get away from you? You almost lost me five hundred feet of prime lumber!" he shouted at his son.

The muscles in Mr. Green's jaw tightened. His eyes narrowed. He stepped down from the wagon. He was slightly taller than Bigjim and in his fine gray suit, he was an imposing figure.

"Mr. Houston, your son was almost killed. He did a fine job of handling the team until the train spooked them. When the reins fell, he needed help. The horses were running like hell to beat tanbark," Mr. Green was almost shouting at Bigjim. He stood boot to boot with Littlejim's father.

Littlejim had never seen anybody shout at Bigjim, not even Uncle Bob. He thought Mr. Green must be a very brave man to dare to shout at his papa. Bigjim took a step backward. His eyes narrowed, but he spoke carefully, as if he was not sure what Mr. Green would do.

"I'm much obliged to you, Mr. Green, for saving my load. I'll take care of tanning the boy's hide when we get home," said Bigjim.

Mr. Green reached up and slapped Littlejim's shoulder. "Fine job, my boy. I'll trade for you instead of that team any day your pa will trade," he said over his shoulder as he walked away.

"Move over, boy. We have to get this lumber unloaded. I'll handle the team," said Bigjim, taking the reins.

"Papa, the train spooked the team. They skipped their traces, and . . ." Littlejim began.

"I don't need no reasons. I saw what happened," said his father. "I told Bob I shouldn't bring you . . ." his voice faded.

Neither of them spoke again until Sam McKinney called Bigjim into the station. Littlejim sat on the lumber and closed his eyes.

"I wish the earth would just open up and swallow me," said Littlejim under his breath as his eyes filled with tears of embarrassment and sadness.

"You hungry, son?" said a voice beside him.

Mr. Green stood there. On a piece of white butcher paper he held two slabs of yellow hoop cheese and a pile of thick white soda crackers.

The man climbed up, sat down and spread the picnic on the seat between them. Then he reached into the pocket of his fine jacket and pulled out another white packet.

"Mr. Price's finest salt pickles. You like salt pickles?" Mr. Green asked.

Littlejim nodded. He bit into the cheese and crackers.

Chapter Eighteen

As he ate, Littlejim began to feel better.

"What does a fine young man like you do when he's not chasing around this town with a load of lumber?" asked Mr. Green.

"I go to school," said Littlejim between bites, "and I'm the dust doodler at Uncle Bob's sawmill on Saturday. I build things out of wood and I help Mama with the chores. I keep hoping Papa will be proud of me, but I can't seem to please him. He still thinks I'm not much of a man and . . ." His words came faster until they were all run together. "And I want to win the essay contest so my words will be printed in the *Star,* and maybe Papa will think . . ."

"Whoa, slow down. You *are* a smart young man. So your papa doesn't think you're the man you should be. Is that it?"

"Yes, sir. No matter what I do, Papa doesn't think

130

it's as good as he could do it, and I want more than anything to prove that I am a man he can be proud of."

Littlejim found himself telling the man about Bigjim and the pictures he saw in his mind and ideas he had about what it means to be an American. Then he told Mr. Green about Mr. McGuire's death and how Lilac had destroyed the tobacco patch he planted for his father. At last he explained about the July Fourth celebration and the essay contest and why he wanted to win.

"Most of all, if Papa sees my words in his *Kansas City Star,* maybe he will be proud of me. I want to win the ten-dollar prize to buy some horses so I can go to the woods like Papa, but Mama says the prize money could be used to send me away to school, so I can be a scholar, like Mr. Osk says I am," said Littlejim.

"Which do you really want, son?" asked the man.

"I really like to learn and to read, but Papa thinks a man should work in the woods and farm and chew tobacco . . ." said the boy. "I always thought I would be a logger, but I really think I would like to go to school."

"Ha!" said Mr. Green. "Well, son, men have different talents. A scholar is as much of a man as a lumberman. You should do what you feel is your own best work."

No one in his life had been so interested in what Littlejim had to say except Mama. He talked on.

"I was working on my essay when the horses got away," he said. "Here, I'll show you." He felt inside his pockets, then picked up his coat and checked there.

"They're gone," he said. "All my pages. Mama gave me the last pages of her tablet paper. They must have dropped off when the horses ran. I lost all my words. And that was the last page of Mama's writing tablet." Littlejim did not feel much like a fine young man just then. His eyes stung with tears of disappointment. "Now I'll never win the competition. I won't have my words printed in the *Star*. And I have failed. I'm just a no-account boy, like Papa said."

The tears threatened to spill over onto his cheeks, but he dared not let them fall.

"What was your essay about?" asked Mr. Green.

"I was writing about what it means to be an American. I thought the words Mr. McGuire said that day he was killed were good ones. He said he came here with nothing, but now he had a home and family. He wanted his bones to rest in American soil."

"Well, I guess most of us or some of our grandparents came here from somewhere else. That's what this country is all about. We all came here as strangers and made this our home," said Mr. Green.

"That's what the man who runs the saw said and Uncle Bob, too," said Littlejim. "He told me his grandfather hid in a barrel on a ship to come here, and Uncle Bob said our grandfather was going to be hanged, like a horse thief." Littlejim found himself laughing at that. Mr. Green laughed, too.

"It's my opinion that many of us started to this land only one step ahead of the sheriff or the hangman," laughed Mr. Green, slapping his thigh. "My grandmother was put into debtors' prison in England for stealing bread for her children when her husband was killed and her money was stolen from her. She was sent to Georgia. She started all over and made a home. She helped her new husband make a fortune there."

"I think that's what I will write about," said Littlejim, thoughtfully nibbling the last of his salt pickle. "I think maybe that's what being an American means, not fighting in a war, or wearing soldiering clothes. Maybe being an American means coming to a new land as strangers and making it our home. Like the Creek is our home."

Suddenly, it all seemed to make sense, just like it had that day when he and Mama planted the tobacco bed. Now he was sure what his essay would say, even though he had lost his papers.

"My boy, I think you have your essay already written," said Mr. Green.

Bigjim stepped up to the wagon at that moment. "You pestering this man, Jimmy," said his father, frowning. He looked as if he wanted to say something to Mr. Green but dared not.

"No, sir," interrupted Mr. Green. "I was pestering *him*. Asking him about Bob's new circle saw at the mill. I've not laid eyes on Bob in years," said Mr. Green. Bigjim was still frowning.

"Fine son you have there, Jim. Had a son like that myself years ago," he continued. Mr. Green looked away. "Typhoid epidemic," his voice was only a choked whisper.

Bigjim ignored Mr. Green and looked away.

"Sam's waiting for us to unload," said Bigjim, gruffly. "Can you bring the team closer to the siding?" He walked over toward the siding.

Mr. Green helped Littlejim position the wagon, then he said, "Good day, son," and walked off across the buggy tracks in the muddy street.

Littlejim helped his father unfasten the chains and climbed on top of the load of lumber to hand the boards down one by one to the men who stacked them into the railcars. As he lifted the boards, his mind began to form words in rhythm to his movements. "They started all over. They made a new home. They started all over. They made a new home . . ."

134

When the wagon was empty, Littlejim guided it back into the street and prepared to follow Bigjim's lead up the hill to River Road.

A voice called from the sidewalk, "Jimmy. Jimmy, wait."

Littlejim reined in the horses. Mr. Green came running up to the side of the wagon. He handed a parcel wrapped in brown paper to the boy.

"Good luck in the essay competition. I'll watch for your words in the *Star*. If you win, I'll come to the July Fourth celebration to hear your speech. Good-bye, son." Mr. Green said.

The man shook Littlejim's hand. Then he slapped Swain's massive rump.

"Giddiup," he said.

Littlejim drove the horses hard to catch up before Bigjim missed him. The wagon was much easier to handle now that the load was gone.

When they had left the town behind, the horses plodded along, following the lead of Bigjim's team. Littlejim opened the parcel. It contained a lined tablet of writing paper and a fat yellow pencil.

Littlejim grinned. No student at the Henson Creek school had ever had anything so fine with which to write his lessons. He placed the package inside his folded coat so Bigjim would not see it.

As they traveled back on the River Road, he

135

thought about how grateful he was to Mr. Green for helping him handle Scott and Swain, and about all the people like him who had made this land their home, and about his home on the Creek that Mama filled with love, no matter what Bigjim said.

Chapter Nineteen

The spring rains came and the daffodils bloomed. With the warm days, students at Mr. Osk's school left their shoes and stockings behind and trekked the Creek road in bare feet. The end of the school year was near.

"That's a prize-winning essay, Jimmy," said Mr. Osk when Littlejim showed him his work.

"I hope my papa will think so," said Littlejim.

Mr. Osk peered at Littlejim through his thick glasses with wire rims.

"Jimmy, I know your papa well. A harder working man never lived. Honest, too. He wants you to better yourself."

Mr. Osk placed a thin hand on Littlejim's shoulder.

"Just last week, he says to me, 'Osk,' says he, 'I could do a lot more if I had that boy in the woods.

137

But to my way a figgerin', he ought to be in school. I didn't get much schooling. He has a good head on his shoulders. I'm bound he'll get more'n I got.' Now, Jimmy, a man that feels that way, he'll be proud if you win the competition."

Littlejim kicked his toe against the porch rail and looked away.

"It appears that I don't do nothing to suit him," said Littlejim. "I got sick the day the gaffer got killed at the mill. I had to leave the butchering when I lost my breakfast. I let the horses run away from me when we went to town. Papa says I ain't much of a man, just a no-account boy."

"Of course you're not much of a man," replied Mr. Osk, with a little snort of a laugh that upset his glasses.

He took them off and blew on them. Then he took a big handkerchief out of his pocket, wiped them and set them on his nose again. Littlejim felt a stinging in his eyes. He blinked. He must not let Mr. Osk see tears. He had always thought Mr. Osk liked him. But now he knew. Mr. Osk felt just like Papa did. The boy's shoulders fell as he turned to walk away.

"Jimmy," asked Mr. Osk. "Where are you going? We're not finished."

Littlejim turned to face Mr. Osk again.

138

"What I was about to say was this. Of course, you're not a man. Not yet. No twelve-year-old boy is yet a man. There's no shame in that. Bigjim demands a lot of you."

"He wants me to be a man. I try, but I can't," said Littlejim. "Everything I do is wrong."

"It just appears that way, my boy," said his teacher. "I seem to remember about your age when every time I walked, I tripped over my own two feet. That's part of life, I reckon," Mr. Osk laughed.

Littlejim laughed, too. Mr. Osk, it was said on the Creek, was the best dancer in these parts. Tripping over his own feet did not seem to be a problem for him now.

"Jimmy, you've the makings of a fine man," said Mr. Osk. "I'd venture a guess that you'll not be a whole lot like Bigjim. It's my guess, you'll be a whole lot more like Bob. He'd be a fine feller to be like, don't you think?" Mr. Osk slapped Littlejim on the shoulder. Littlejim grinned.

"I don't know anybody I'd rather be like than Uncle Bob," he said.

"Now, Jimmy, I'm of a mind that it may be that Bigjim is a mite envious of his fine son. That son has a good mind and can do so many things well. That fine son has a way with words. He can work with his hands and he's my prize pupil in this school. Bigjim's a fine man, but you can do a number of things he can't do."

Littlejim blushed. "Thank you, Mr. Osk," he said. Littlejim had never thought there was anything his papa couldn't do. Then he remembered the struggle his father had to read the words in the *Star* or the almanac. Reading was an easy thing for his son to do.

"I don't think you need to worry anymore about being a man. And a fine man you'll be when the time comes. Don't you fret."

"I hope I can show Papa that I am," said Littlejim, with a sigh.

Mr. Osk led the boy back into the schoolroom.

Every day while the other students played outside, Littlejim sat at his desk studying and revising his essay.

He read half aloud, "Being an American means we can start all over when we fail . . ." Then he wrote about Lilac and the tobacco bed and all the people he had heard about who started all over and how they had made the new land their home.

Through the door, he could hear the chant:

"William a Trimmy Toe,
He's a good fisherman.
He catches hens,
Puts them in pens.
Some lay eggs,

140

Some lay none.
William a Trimmy Toe,
He's a good fisherman.
Wire, briar, limber lock,
Three geese in a flock.
One flew east,
One flew west,
One flew over the cuckoo's nest,
Wire, briar, limber lock."

While his classmates played the circle game, their voices echoing a chant, Littlejim revised his essay, sometimes reading it aloud to hear the rhythm of the words.

Finally, it was ready to present for the end of school ceremonies.

Chapter Twenty

It was May and the last day of school had arrived.
Parents had come to listen to the recitations and essays prepared by the students in Mr. Osk's school.

Mama was seated at Nell's desk, holding Baby
May. Mr. and Mrs. Vance had seats of honor near the
black stove as did the preacher. As the students presented their recitations, the parents applauded po-
litely.

Andy McGuire quietly shook hands with Littlejim
behind his desk. "Good luck," he said. "I hope you
win." His freckled face was red with hoping for his
friend.

Ivor Vance leaned across the aisle and nudged
Littlejim's arm. "I hate to see a younger fellow win,
but since I didn't enter, I guess I'm happy you're sure
to win the prize." He laughed, then leaned back and
crossed his arms.

"Boys, boys," said Mr. Osk. "It is time for silence. Our competition will begin. We will draw numbers to determine the order in which your essays will be delivered."

Littlejim drew the highest number, which meant he had to wait until everyone else had read. One by one the pupils in Mr. Osk's class walked to the platform and read their essays.

Finally, it was Littlejim's turn. As he stood up to read his essay, he smiled at Mama. She smiled back. She had helped him practice every day that Bigjim was late in the woods.

"He will learn of his son's triumph when the time is right," she said. "It is not unusual for his son to recite at the school, so if he hears about your recitation at the close of school ceremonies, he will think nothing of it."

Littlejim pushed his hair back out of his eyes and wiped his sweaty hands on his new pants. He really wanted to win this competition.

He began to read, "I think that what it means to be an American is that this land is our home. It was not always so. Almost all of us came from someplace else. Our ancestors left their homes and came to build a new land. Now that new land is our home, just like the Creek is home to all of us who live there.

"The man who first gave me the idea of what it

means to be an American came from somewhere else. His name was Adam McGuire and he came here from Ireland. He made the Creek his home. He worked at my Uncle Bob's sawmill. One day he told us at noonday dinner, 'This land's been mighty good to me. I came here with nothing in my pockets. Now I have land, a home and a fine family. This is a good land.'

"And Mr. Wiseman told us how his grandfather hid in a tobacco hogshead on a ship that sailed over the ocean. He didn't have any money, so he served as an indentured servant to pay for his passage. He came here and made it his home. To Mr. Wiseman, this was a good land, too."

He read on. He read of the first Houston who ran like a horse thief and he read of Mr. Green's grandmother. He read of his own grandfather who knew he was an American when he began to count in English. He read of all the people he had heard about who came from someplace else to make their homes in this new land.

Finally, he read, ". . . and most of all, being an American means we live in a place where a man or a woman or a boy or a girl, can start over when we fail, like I started over when Lilac destroyed the tobacco bed."

When he had finished, the parents applauded

loudly. Littlejim bowed, smiled and sat down. Mr. Osk called a recess. The students and their visitors wandered out to the school grounds.

"Do you think I will win?" Littlejim whispered to Mama.

"Yours was the best essay I have heard today," said Mama. "But then I am partial to my fine son's work, so perhaps I am not a good judge of its quality."

"You'll win," said Nell. "I know you will, Little-jim."

Mr. Osk rang his handbell to call everyone back to the schoolroom, and then asked Littlejim, Jo Rhyne, Sam Barrier, and Carl Hicks to come to the platform. Littlejim held his breath.

"Fourth place, Carl Hicks," he said, shaking hands with the tallest boy in the class.

"Third place, Jo Rhyne," he said, bowing to the smiling girl.

That left only Littlejim and Sam Barrier standing.

Mr. Vance stood up and took a small box from Mrs. Vance. "I will announce second place and the winner," he said. "Sam Barrier."

Littlejim swallowed hard. He had not won.

"Second place," continued Mr. Vance. "Now for the entry in the competition at the *Kansas City Star*. Jimmy Houston, first place." He turned to Littlejim and then shook hands with each winner.

Littlejim's face broke into a grin so wide he felt his face would break. His spirits lifted. He smiled at Mama and shook hands with the others.

The sun had never shone brighter on Henson Creek than the joy in Littlejim's face that day. Maybe Papa could see his words in the *Star* after all.

Chapter Twenty-one

Now that school was out, Bigjim expected the children to take over most of the farm work. The cornfield had to be plowed with the big double-shovel plow between the rows, while the weeds were removed within the long rows of corn by Mama, Nell and Banjer Brown when he was available.

Sometimes, when the hoeing was finished, the children were sent to gather the early wild greens for cooking. Littlejim and Nell were careful to gather only the young tender shoots of the poke plant for "poke sallet," which Mama withered with ham drippings. The older shoots were poisonous. Dandelion greens were also a delicacy to be prized after the long winter with only cabbage as a green vegetable.

The chickens hatched little "dibs" and Nell chased the tiny yellow birds around the chickenyard, trying to catch them. Old Jerse gave birth to a new calf, and soon there was plenty of fresh milk and rich yellow butter. All the world of the Creek seemed to be blooming with new life.

Soon it was time for the first cutting of hay for the year. Bigjim took time from the woods to ride the mower pulled by Scott and Swain. Littlejim and Banjer used the scythes along the edges of the meadows. After the hay had dried, the men of the neighborhood joined Bigjim to rake and stack the hay into big haystacks near the barns and in the corner of the pasture.

Then the Transparent apples were ripe. Mama and the children gathered them, peeled them and made applesauce or dried them on wire racks hung over the cookstove in the kitchen. A few weeks later the cherries were ripe and had to be picked.

And almost every day, the hoeing of one field or another, and sometimes in Mama's vegetable garden, had to be done. Littlejim and Nell complained and wore blisters from the hoe handles. But each time they complained, Mama reminded them that if the family was to eat during the winter, the crops must be made in the summer.

Sometimes, Littlejim slipped off to tend his new small tobacco patch hidden away in the clearing he had made in the laurel thicket, where Bigjim seldom went. The tobacco was growing well, and Littlejim thought he would have a surprise for his father in the fall, if Bigjim didn't stumble on the secret garden.

But Littlejim and Nell found time to have some fun. Mama insisted that the children go fishing and swimming. Sometimes she and Baby May went with them. As the weather grew warmer, the meat in the smokehouse dwindled and fried fish provided a tasty supper. Littlejim and Nell cut birch poles and tied fishing line to them. Then they dug up red worms and caught grasshoppers for bait. The creek was filled with trout, red bellies and the horny-heads that were hardly fit to eat. Best of their catch were the speckled trout. Nell usually caught more of them than her brother.

The times Littlejim and Nell liked best were when Bigjim was still in the woods and Mama joined them on the creek bank with her black frying pan to cook the fish outdoors. Bigjim thought cooking outdoors belonged to hunting trips and church singings. He wanted his daily "rations," as he called them, cooked in his house on the finest cookstove on the Creek. But when he was away overnight, Mama often cooked the children's catch down by the creek.

Mama would roll the fish in corn meal ground from corn grown in their own fields and fry it in bacon fat. Littlejim would dig new potatoes and bury them in the ashes to roast. The last of the cornmeal was formed into hoecakes and cooked after the fish were ready to eat. The food tasted so much better than it did even in Mama's kitchen.

Some evenings Mr. Osk came over to join them. He and Mama laughed as they cleaned the fish, remembering the days when as children living in the same house they had fished and cooked on this same creek bank.

Occasionally, Andy McGuire was allowed to leave his chores and join them. Sometimes Dr. Shoop would stop by in his buggy to allow Emma to join Nell in wading in the creek. Once Andy and Littlejim caught tadpoles and dropped them from the tree limb above as the girls waded in the shallow water. Mama was not pleased with Littlejim's manners that day. He and Andy were not allowed to share the sweet cakes Mama had brought to end the meal until they apologized for frightening the younger children.

And every time Mr. Osk came to eat fish with them, Littlejim always asked the same question: "Have you heard from the essay competition yet?"

But Mr. Osk always had the same answer. "Not yet, Jimmy."

Chapter Twenty-two

Mama's basket sat on the front porch filled to the brim with fried chicken, potato salad and fried apple pies. A wild-strawberry cake hid under a dishpan. Alongside the basket was one black iron pot of green beans and ham with new potatoes fresh from the garden, and another filled with sweet yellow kernels of the summer's first "ros' nears." A smaller basket of ripe tomatoes and cucumbers for slicing sat nearby, and a frosty brown crock held lemonade, sweetened with honey.

Everything was ready for the July Fourth celebration in the meadow on top of the mountain called the Grassy Ridge Bald. July Fourth was the one celebration Bigjim firmly believed in. Most years he won the men's wrestling contest, the horseshoe pitching and the footrace. The rest of the year he didn't believe in celebrating, but come July Fourth, Bigjim was, as he said, "raring to go."

The sun was getting hot as Mama came through the front door with the fanlight over it. She was carrying Baby May.

"Littlejim," said Nell, struggling to load the basket into the wagon. "Help me with the big basket. Mama says not to let the potato salad turn over." But Littlejim was practicing his throwing arm for the horseshoe pitching contest.

"I'll be there in a minute," her brother called. "As soon as I finish."

"Mama says to come right now," said Nell. "She wants to get there in time for the preaching and the speeches."

Nell left the basket to come over to whisper in her brother's ear. "Are you going to read your essay? Does Papa know?"

"Yes, I'm going to read my essay, but Papa doesn't know anything about it."

"Do you think he'll be mad?" asked Nell.

"Mr. Osk thinks he will be proud of me," said Littlejim.

"Did you win?" she asked.

"I don't know if I won or not. I have looked every week in Papa's *Star*. My essay hasn't been printed, but I haven't seen another."

"I hope you do," she added. "I don't want you to get a whipping tonight."

Littlejim was frightened that Bigjim would disapprove of his reading the essay, but he wanted to appear brave and manly for his little sister. "Don't worry," he said. "Mr. Osk says everything will be all right. Help me with these horseshoes."

Nell helped him gather the horseshoes, carefully selected for balance from Bigjim's tack room in the barn. Littlejim tied them with a short rope and dropped them into the corner of the box wagon. Scott and Swain stamped their feet, eager to be on their way.

"What do you want to load first?" Littlejim asked his sister.

"Here it is," Nell answered. "By the wagon."

Mama came down the steps. She was dressed in her Sunday-go-to-meeting clothes, a flowered dress of lawn with a fresh white collar and cuffs. Her skirt was covered with a starched white apron. She carried Baby May, who chewed on a sugar-babe made of a square of clean cloth tied tightly around a lump of brown sugar.

"May, don't drop that on your dress," said Nell, as she searched her pockets for a clean handkerchief to wipe her sister's chin.

Bigjim came around the side of the house from the field in back. He had dressed up for the occasion. He wore his best brown pants held up with new suspenders and stuffed into his high logging boots. His starched white collar held his chin high in the air, so his brown beard jutted out in front of him.

"Where his beard leads him, Papa will follow," sang Nell under her breath, using the melody of the hymn, "Where He leads me, I will follow."

But Littlejim heard. "Better not let Papa hear you funning him!" whispered her brother. Nell knew better than to let Papa hear her making a funny song from the hymn he liked to sing when he went to church on a rare Sunday.

But Bigjim had stopped at the edge of the porch. Littlejim looked up into eyes that flashed like lightning. His heart almost stopped from fear. The tall man reached out to grab Littlejim's arm. Mama took a step toward her son.

"I've just been out to the garden. What do you mean, growing tobaccer behind my back? I found your secret place, boy, and now I know you're a-smoking and a-chewing behind my back!" Bigjim spat the words at his son.

"But, Papa . . ." Mama moved quickly to stand between father and son. She raised her arms as if to ward off blows. Bigjim took a step back.

"I don't want to hear none of your lip, you no-account boy! What else you been doing behind my back?" A voice interrupted him.

"Jim, he was growing that tobaccer for you. I gave

155

him the plants. Now let that boy go," Cousin Tarp walked up the hill and into the yard. He walked slowly over to Littlejim and removed Bigjim's hand from the boy's arm. Mama stepped back.

"Jim, you never did learn to think before you spoke, or acted, for that matter," said Tarp. "This boy's planning for you to have your chaw come winter. I don't think that's cause for striking him, now, do you?"

Bigjim did not respond. He turned and disappeared into the woodshed. The lump in Littlejim's throat stayed until Mama quickly said, "The singing's begun already. Load this food. Be on our way, we'd best be."

Finally, the wagon was loaded. Littlejim lifted Nell to sit on the back beside the food baskets. Then he swung himself up beside her. His legs, long for their twelve years, dangled beside Nell's short ones. His dusty bare feet almost touched the green grass of the front yard. Nell's bare toes were still clean from her Saturday bath.

Littlejim turned his head away to stare at the roof of the springhouse down the hill so his little sister could not see the tears in his eyes. Nell moved closer to her brother. She patted his arm.

"I'm sorry Papa is so mean to you, Littlejim," she whispered.

156

"Seems like I can't do anything to suit him. What's the use in trying?" he whispered, working hard to squeeze the words past the lump in his throat.

"Well, I love you and Mama loves you. And Cousin Tarp and Uncle Bob and Mr. Osk likes you best of all because you are so smart. We all love you. Please don't be sad," said his sister. "It's July Fourth and that's a happy day." She smiled and handed her brother a clean handkerchief from her apron pocket.

Littlejim blew his nose and continued to stare at the springhouse roof. "Much obliged," he said.

Mama, Baby May and Cousin Tarp sat on the seat at the front of the wagon. As Cousin Tarp giddiupped the horses, Bigjim walked back into the yard. Cousin Tarp handed the reins to him and moved in silence to the back of the wagon to sit between Littlejim and Nell. He threw an arm around Littlejim and one around Nell. He gave their shoulders a squeeze. Scott and Swain stepped off in unison. Littlejim grabbed the side of the wagon with one hand as the wagon moved forward.

"We're off to the all-day singing and dinner on the ground!" shouted Cousin Tarp.

The horses made their way up the mountain. As the steep climb began, they passed the Freewill Church. As they rounded the bend of the road,

Littlejim could see the cemetery. Although the flowers had begun to fade from the Sunday past, the graves were still a blaze of color. The gray tombstones stood guard over baskets and earthenware jugs of flowers specially grown in family gardens for Decoration Day—homecoming for all the kith and kin of the church. Some of the oblong graves were entirely covered with flowers arranged in a design on the grass. He could see some of the crepe paper flowers that he, Mama and Nell had made and placed on the graves of near kin on Decoration Day.

Littlejim liked the family gathering of Decoration Day, but it was a solemn occasion with much visiting on the part of the grownups. He liked the July Fourth celebration better. On Decoration Day, he and all the others his age had to sit quietly through sermons and hymn singing, but at July Fourth, there were games and competitions. He could hardly wait to get to the top of the Grassy Ridge Bald where the celebration would be held.

As the horses climbed the steep road, Littlejim checked the back pocket of his pants to be sure the tablet pages where he had written his essay were safely tucked away there. As he touched the papers, he began to feel better.

"Surely Papa will like my speech and when he hears it, then he will be proud of me," he thought. But with Papa, you never knew.

Chapter Twenty-three

Scott and Swain strained their huge muscles as they pulled the wagon up the last steep incline through the trees to the top of Grassy Ridge Bald. Suddenly the trees were behind them, and a flat meadow lay in front of them. Littlejim could see the green waves of the long bladed grass, called bald grass because it grew only in the treeless meadows on the tops of the the high mountains. He thought it looked like an ocean.

The cool air felt fresh against his skin. The wind blew constantly up from the west and across the mountaintop. Littlejim loved to jump and run in the wind. Its buoyancy lifted him higher than he could run and jump anyplace else. He wondered if he took a big runny-go, maybe he could leap high enough to touch the sky.

Bigjim tied the horses to a rhododendron some folks called red laurel. It was now bursting into full bloom so deeply red it was almost purple. The family unloaded the wagon. Around the edge of the grounds, residents from Henson Creek on the east side of the mountain and from Cane Creek on the west side of the mountain, as well as people from all the communities nearby, gathered in their Sunday-go-to-meeting best. They stood around in groups, sharing the news of the year since they had seen one another last.

At the highest point in the meadow, tables had been made of boards set on saw horses. Those tables held the best that the gardens and kitchens of the Blue Ridge Mountains had to offer. Littlejim's mouth watered at the thought as he helped Mama and Nell spread the bounty they had brought in the wagon. Near the end of the tables, fires had been started to warm the vegetables which were to be served hot, like green beans and potatoes, and "ros' nears," and to make the coffee demanded at any social gathering.

On the south side of the meadow, standing so the sun was not in their eyes, were the massed choirs from all the churches in the surrounding countryside. The singing master "do-sol-me-doed" and the singing began. Then Preacher Hall began his sermon. It was shorter than the sermons at church on Sunday, but Littlejim's back grew tired and his stomach began to remind him that breakfast had been many hours ago.

His thoughts wandered to where Bigjim sat with the men gathered in a corner of the meadow by themselves. There they felt free when moved to shout "Amen" in accordance with the preacher's words. He wondered if his papa would be mad enough to whip him for reading his essay. He was glad that Cousin Tarp had come up the hill at the right moment that morning. Papa had been mighty upset about the tobacco bed hidden in the woods.

"I guess I am just a no-account boy, but everybody except Papa seems to think I'm all right. Why doesn't he think so, too?" Littlejim whispered.

"Sh-h-h! Littlejim," whispered Nell. "The preacher is talking. Mama wants us to mind our manners."

The preacher finished his sermon and the choirmaster motioned for everyone to stand.

"It is time for me to join the men in singing," said Littlejim to Nell. He turned and walked over to the group of men. Uncle Bob shook hands with Littlejim and made a place between himself and Tarp for the boy. Mr. Osk slapped him on the back and shook his hand, too. Ivor, Carl Hicks and Andy McGuire stood in a line with some of the younger boys in front of the men.

The women sang, "When the roll . . ."

The men echoed, "When the roll . . ." Littlejim could feel his voice deepen to join the men.

". . . is called up yonder . . ." sang the women.

". . . is called up yonder . . ." echoed the men.

Then everyone sang together, "When the roll is called up yonder, I'll be there . . ."

"I'll be there," echoed the men.

When the singing was finished, Preacher Hall invited a visiting preacher from Cane Creek to return thanks.

"Almighty God," the voice began.

Littlejim's stomach was grumbling loudly by the time the prayer was finished. Finally it was time to eat. Nell came skipping across the meadow hand in hand with her friend, Emma. Annie Burleson was trying hard to keep up with the older girls. They circled up with three little girls from the Cane Creek community to play "Jenny Jenkins" while the adults lined up to eat.

First, the preacher and all the men heaped their plates high. Then the women served plates for all the older folks who sat on a pew from the Missionary Church. Then the children could fill their plates, too. Last of all, the women who had cooked the food through the long week just passed could eat their fill as they tended the babies and caught up on the news from the past year.

Slowly the men and boys slipped away to begin their games and competitions. The visiting preacher would tender another sermon in one corner of the

Bald field, but only the old folks would stay to listen.

Littlejim helped Mama pack away the empty dishes. Mama's food was always the most popular at any dinner on the ground. Most of the bowls were empty. Only crumbs remained of the wild-strawberry cake. He hadn't even had a bite of it, so he scraped the crumbs from the plate and poured them into his mouth. When he had loaded the baskets, pots and pans into the wagon, he grabbed the horseshoes and headed for the horseshoe pitching contest.

Bigjim, wiry and thin, but strong from his days in the woods, was wrestling Moose Winters from Cane Creek. Littlejim stopped to watch with Andy McGuire. The boys yelled for Bigjim as the tall man pinned the heavier one to the ground and was announced the winner.

"Your pa sure is strong," said Andy. "My pa would not . . ." He stopped and turned away from his friend. Littlejim remembered the cold day Andy's father had fallen into the saw at the sawmill.

Littlejim slapped his friend on the arm. "Come on. Let's go enter the horseshoe throwing." But inside he wondered how Andy felt since he had no papa. "I guess a papa who doesn't like you is better than no papa at all," he thought.

He walked past Bigjim. "I'm proud of you, Papa," said the boy.

"Just remember that," his father answered, buttoning up his shirt. Then Bigjim turned away and walked toward the wagon.

The horseshoe pitching competition for the boys Littlejim's age was to begin. Andy went first. His aim was good. Then several other boys took their turn.

Littlejim's first pitch was true, but he stepped up to pitch his second shoe when everyone turned away to look. Littlejim lost his aim, and the pitch fell shy.

Coming across the meadow was the Vances' fine automobile pulled by Uncle Bob's team. Uncle Bob rode astride Shilo's back. Everyone laughed.

"Get a horse," shouted one of the Cane Creek men.

The Vances stepped down from the car.

"The horseshoe pitching contest is over," announced Mr. Osk. "Andy McGuire is the winner."

Littlejim was happy for his friend, but felt his own disappointment keenly at losing because his father usually won at horseshoes. Then Mr. Vance asked, "Are you ready to give your speech, Jimmy?"

"Yessir," the boy answered. His hands began to sweat and his hair fell into his eyes.

"The *Star* hasn't come yet this week, but if you had won, we would have had a letter from them before now. I'm sorry you didn't win the first prize from the *Star,* but we are still proud of you, Jimmy," said Mr. Vance.

Littlejim's eyes stung as he faced the sun. Now Papa would really be mad at him for writing the essay and for making a plumb fool of himself by reading it. Now he would never see his words printed in the *Star*. Papa would never understand why he had written the essay.

He wanted to run away, but Mr. Vance said, "Well, my boy. It is time to read your essay."

Littlejim swallowed hard and walked toward the rock that served as a speaker's platform. He looked at the sky. A dark cloud had covered the sun.

Chapter Twenty-four

Mr. Vance stood beside Littlejim on the speaker's rock. Littlejim took the essay out of his pocket as Mr. Vance announced his speech.

"Mrs. Vance and I at T. B. Vance's store in Plumtree, North Carolina," he took a little bow, "announced a competition last January. The competition was for an essay written on the subject, 'What it means to be an American,' a good subject for a July Fourth speech, we believe. The winner presented his essay at the end of school recitations at Mr. Osk's school on Henson Creek. Then we entered the winning essay in a competition of the winners from twelve states at the *Kansas City Star*. The *Star* offered a ten-dollar prize and they will publish the winning essay."

Littlejim wished the man would hurry and finish so he could read. He could see Bigjim standing near the wagons, his arms folded across his chest and his slouch hat pulled low over his eyes. Trying to stop his hands from shaking, Littlejim stuck one hand into his pocket. Andy McGuire waved at him from the front row of the crowd gathered to hear the speeches. He managed to smile at Andy.

"The winner of the essay contest from Mr. Osk's school was Jimmy Houston, Littlejim, son of Bigjim and Gertrude Houston. We're mighty sorry he didn't win the *Star* contest, too, but we're real proud of him anyway. He is going to read his essay to us now."

Littlejim took his hand out of his pocket and tried to still the paper, which was shaking violently in spite of the hot sun warming his hands. He began to read. As he lost himself in his words, his shaking calmed and his voice grew stronger.

". . . and most of all, being an American means we live in a place where a man or a woman or a boy or a girl, can start over when we fail, like I started over when Lilac destroyed the tobacco bed I planted for my papa. It means living in a place where, although we come from somewhere else, we can call home, a place where we belong, a place like my home on Henson Creek in North Carolina in the shadow of Spear Tops Mountain, where my papa, my mama, my sisters and I live. We are all Americans because this is the place where we belong. Here we have all come home."

But Littlejim barely got to read the last sentence of the essay. A rider on a large gray horse came thundering across the bald grass. The rider wore a gray suit and a fine gray hat. He pulled in the reins at the speaker's rock and jumped from the saddle.

Mr. George G. Green, owner of the livery stable in Spruce Pine, held a newspaper in his hand. His saddlebags were stuffed with more newspapers.

"Hold everything," Mr. Green announced. "This week's *Star* just arrived at the railroad station in town this morning. Sam McKinney asked me if I would ride up to the gathering with it. I came as fast as I could."

The group of people gathered around the field moved closer to the speaker's rock. Mr. Green held up the newspaper.

"Right here on the front page is the winning essay for the competition. The winning essay is from Mr. Osk's school on Henson Creek, sponsored by T. B. Vance's store in Plumtree. The winning essay was written by Jimmy Houston," he said.

The men and boys burst into applause. Littlejim blushed. He looked at Mama. She was smiling and her face shone with pride. Nell and her friends were jumping up and down, clapping their hands. "Littlejim's best! Littlejim's best," they shouted.

"And here is a letter from the *Star* addressed to

Mr. Vance. If I were a betting man, I'd say it is a letter informing us that Jimmy is the winner," continued Mr. Green.

Mr. Vance took the letter and opened it. A small tan paper fluttered to the ground. Mr. Vance picked it up.

"A check for ten dollars, made out to Jimmy Houston," announced Mr. Vance.

The crowd applauded again. Mr. Vance shook hands with Littlejim and handed him the check. Littlejim stared at it. He had never seen so much money. Mr. Green shook hands with Littlejim, too.

Then the man in the gray suit walked back to his horse and took the copies of the *Kansas City Star* out of his saddlebags. He called the names of the men who received the newspaper each week. One by one they claimed their papers and walked away, shaking their heads in wonder that the words of one of their own were printed there.

Finally, Mr. Green called out, "James Houston."

Bigjim unfolded his arms and walked toward the speaker's rock, his head down, his face hidden beneath the brim of his slouch hat. He took the paper from Mr. Green and turned to leave, still not looking at his son.

Mr. Osk looked at Uncle Bob, and he walked over to take Bigjim's arm. "Jim, you must be the proudest man on the Creek," he said.

170

Uncle Bob took Bigjim's other arm. "Jim, what a wonder you have produced in that boy! His words printed right there in the *Star*."

Mr. Green spoke. His voice commanded attention. "A man would have to be mighty proud to be the sire of a boy who can write such powerful words. Yes, I reckon he's much of a man." He turned to Littlejim. "I reckon the writer of such powerful words is much of a man, too."

Bigjim turned to face his son. Littlejim could barely see his eyes under the slouch hat brim. "Well, I reckon, if his words are important enough for the *Star* to print, they must be powerful important." He opened the paper and stared at the words. The tall man's lips formed the words of his son's name.

For a long moment no one moved or spoke. The wind made the only sound.

"I reckon a man that could write such powerful words is right much of a man," said Bigjim. He turned to look at his son. His eyes glistened although they were shaded from the sun by his hat. "Yeah, right much of a man, I guess," he said as he quickly walked away.

The cloud passed from the sun. The light from that sun had never shone brighter. Littlejim felt warm all over as Mr. Green and Uncle Bob lifted him high on their shoulders and carried him around the grounds, followed by the rest of the gathering. Carl and Ivor and Andy gathered in front of the procession to shout "Hip. Hip. Hooray! Littlejim won!" The smaller children followed dancing, singing and shouting.

Bigjim stood to himself away from the others. Mama walked over to her tall husband. She took his arm and stood on tiptoe. Bigjim pointed to his son's name in the newspaper and smiled as he put his arm around Mama. Mama gave him a big hug and looked over at Littlejim, smiling.

At that moment, Littlejim knew that as soon as the men put his feet on the grass, he could leap up and touch the sky.